The Tapu Garden of Eden

A mysterious, moving and uniquely New Zealand story, for sensitive people, young and old, about how the past continues to influence the present.

BY

ROBERT PHILIP BOLTON

Also by Robert Philip Bolton
To The White Gate
My Marian Year
The Boltons of The Little Boltons
Underneath the Arclight
Nana's Special Day and other stories
The Dolphin and other stories
Quickies
The Collected Short Stories
For Viktor. The story of Mussorgsky's 'Pictures at an Exhibition'

Robert Philip Bolton was born in New Zealand in 1945. He has been writing most of his adult life. Most of his work is about New Zealand and New Zealanders. He lives in Auckland.

The Tapu Garden of Eden
A mysterious, moving and uniquely New Zealand story, for sensitive people, young and old, about how the past continues to influence the present.

Author's notes

Maungawhau (Mount Eden) is an extinct volcano formed about twenty thousand years ago. It is the youngest and highest of more than thirty such volcanic cones on the Auckland mainland most of which were used by the ancient Maori to defend their occupation of the narrow and highly desirable isthmus of Auckland they called Tamaki-makaurau. Using tools of wood and stone the defenders sculpted the slopes of these tall hills into wide terraces for gardening, dug trenches and pits at the top for food storage, dwellings and defence, and sometimes erected a perimeter of wooden stockades. The outlines of these remarkable pre-historic excavations, hardly appreciated by the people of New Zealand, are still visible on many of the Auckland peaks including Maungawhau.

Maungawhau means 'the mountain of whau', the whau being a shrub of thin branches *(Entelia Aborescens)* used by the Maori to make fishing nets. The British settlers named it Mount Eden after George Eden, the first Earl of Auckland who was the governor-general of India at the time Auckland was founded.

No doubt the British settlers — who came from a land where the highest 'mountain' was Ben Nevis, a mere 1,343 metres (4,400 feet) — were impressed by the bulk of Maungawhau and its vast pedestal and so had no hesitation in calling it a mountain. But none of the so-called 'mountains' of Auckland is a mountain at all. At 196 metres (650 feet) Mount Eden is dwarfed by New Zealand's real mountains such as Ruapehu (2,797 metres/9,180 feet) in the North Island and the country's tallest mountain, Aorangi (Mount Cook, 3,753 metres/12,300 feet) in the South Island.

There is a sprinkling of Maori words used in this story which will be familiar to New Zealand readers while non-New Zealanders should be able to infer their meaning from the context in which they are used. At least that is my hope. In case I am wrong, and because explanations in the narrative would be unnatural and patronising, I have provided a simple glossary at the back of the book.

The Tapu Garden of Eden is a work of fiction. Although the neighbourhood around Maungawhau is called Mount Eden, and is serviced by Mount Eden Road, there is no Allison Terrace, nothing called Edenside, and no Maungawhau marae. The people too are imaginary although I once knew an old man in Mount Eden much like Olav Kirsten. He had a large garden there, surrounded by a scoria wall, and owned a handsome golden Labrador whose photo hangs above my desk. Any resemblance to any other person, living or dead, is a coincidence.

Robert Philip Bolton
Auckland
June, 2006

Prologue

Long ago a young man arrived in New Zealand from faraway Europe. He was a sailor from Norway. He had travelled the world but had never before been so far from home.

But when, on one cold winter's July day, early in the twentieth century, his little ship steamed down the east coast of Aotearoa (New Zealand) and into the Waitemata harbour of Auckland, he knew he had found the most beautiful country in the world.

"Here I shall stay," he said, in his own language. "I shall make this place my home."

Auckland was not a large city then so the young man was able, with his savings, to buy a small parcel of stony land on the gentle and sunny north-western slopes of Mount Eden, the sleeping volcano that, even today, dominates this beautiful place. Clearing his land of rocks and stones — the better to cultivate its fertile volcanic soil — the young man from Norway came to learn much about the ancient Maori people who once lived on the mountain they still call Maungawhau. Walking on the high slopes above his land he could see the shapes of their terraced gardens, and the hollows that were once dwellings and food storage pits. And he wondered what life was like in those not-so-distant times.

1

He talked often to the old Maori people who then still lived about, especially to the women who seemed to outlast their men and who, in those days, smoked their clay pipes and wore their moko — their chin tattoo — with noble pride. They bought this strange young man's kumara to sell outside the post office. And they talked freely to him about the history of the land he had bought from one of their people, searching their memories of how it once was, because he really wanted to know.

Over many years of digging and hoeing in his garden he found much evidence of Maori history. And when he uncovered something interesting — a fragment of carved bone, perhaps — the people from the university and the museum would come, and he would let them dig and sift through the soft, moist, volcanic earth surrounding his discovery, watching them quietly, and speculating with them on its significance and origin. Thus, slowly, and without realising it, the man from Norway became an expert in the Maori history of Mount Eden, gaining the respect of both the academic and Maori communities of his adopted home.

He lived in a little stone cottage built from the scoria he had cleared from the land. Indeed, he had enough stone to build a wall around his entire garden, where he lived and worked until he was very old, when our story begins.

We meet him, his dog, his young neighbour, and his mysterious friend. And we find out why, many years later, his garden is a park with broad trees, mown lawns, shell walks, and

2

flower beds; why the wall is still there but not the cottage; and why nearby, where there was once a worn dirt path, a black iron fence stands to mark the location of a special grave.

Chapter 1.

"You talk to the plants."

The old man was digging his garden. He straightened up slowly from his work and turned towards the voice. There was a boy in the street, a small boy, standing on the bottom bar of the garden gate. His arms were wrapped around the top of the wickets and he was looking directly at the tall, thin old man.

The man — who had a very wrinkled face, pale blue eyes, a long white beard and long white hair — had seen the boy at the gate before. But the boy had not spoken until now; he appeared happy just to watch the old man, and the old man didn't mind. But now, for the first time, the boy had spoken so the old man stopped his work, pressed his heavy spade into the soil, and walked to the gate to better hear what the boy was saying.

"What you say?" he asked.

"Why do you talk to the plants? Can they hear you?"

"Oh, yes," said the old man whose name was Olav Kirsten. "They can hear. They can hear."

He spoke with a strange accent but the boy didn't seem to notice.

"You are listening?" asked the man curiously. "When I am talking with my beans you are listening?"

The boy nodded. Neither of them spoke again at once but the boy remained on the gate looking freely and slowly at the garden behind the old man. Olav Kirsten wiped his brow with his sleeve and waited, grateful for the short rest.

The boy had seen the garden before and had sensed — as many sensitive children had — that it had a special beauty beyond its appearance. It was quiet there. Its tidiness and tranquillity made people peaceful inside, and kind towards other people, animals and nature. There were many smells: the moist smell of compost and earth; the heavy sweet scent of flowers. There were always birds in the tall trees. And near the old man's cottage, beside his glasshouse, there was a black-looking pond — still and mysterious — where, if they shaded their eyes against the reflections, children could see orange-coloured fish moving lazily through the cool water.

From the gate the boy could see up the middle path, which was wider than the other paths, to the cottage. It was only a small cottage and it stood, at the far edge of the land close to the back boundary which was marked by the scoria stone wall and the grassy-green rising of the great and bulky Maungawhau. Like the garden wall the cottage was made of large scoria stones held together with concrete. The roof was red-painted tin, and there was a yellow brick chimney at one end. Over the single cream-painted door was a tin awning with wooden supports. A green vine with dark red flowers — a *bougainvillaea* — grew wild around the door and over the awning making darkly-dappled shade on the dusty entrance. A wooden chair stood by itself in the shade, and beside the chair lay a large black dog.

The boy smiled when he saw the dog. Then, as he watched, the dog lifted himself heavily — he was evidently an old dog — and, with his head down, padded slowly down the middle path to where the old man was standing.

"There's Brian," said the boy, looking back to the old man.

"Ja. Is Brian. My dog."

"He's a nice dog. Is he *very* old?"

The dog stood faithfully beside Olav Kirsten and blinked slowly as he looked up at the boy on the gate.

"Ja. Is old. Like me is old," said the old man leaning down to rub the dog gently on the head. The dog wagged his tail slowly in response.

"Do you talk to Brian, too?" asked the boy.

"Oh, Ja," replied the man. "Talk to Brian. He understands my words. You understand, Brian, don't you."

The dog turned from the boy to look up at the man. Then he sat down heavily to stare at the boy again.

"Your garden is big," said the boy. "Do you grow all these things on your own?"

"Oh, no," said Olav Kirsten.

"But Hone said you have no one to help you."

Young Hone Wihongi was the old man's neighbour and good friend. He lived with his mother in the house next door.

"Hone said that did he? But there is the sun and the rain and all of nature to help me."

The boy nodded, seeming to understand.

"What is your name?" asked Olav Kirsten.

The boy told him his name.

"You know Hone, Peter?" asked the old man.

"Yes," said the boy.

"You come here with Hone?"

"Yes," said the boy.

"When? Last year?" He was trying to remember the boy.

"Yes," said the boy. "Last year. But sometimes I come and watch you and you don't know. I watch you over the wall, talking to the plants."

"I know. I know. Sometimes I feel you there and I look up and see you," said the old man, grinning. "But why do you watch only, Peter? You should speak to me before this."

"Auntie said you are a good man. She said you have been kind. She told me and I wanted to see you."

The old man was puzzled.

"Who is your auntie, Peter?" he asked. "What is her name?"

The boy shrugged. "Auntie. That's all. She knows you."

Olav Kirsten nodded but he didn't understand.

"I have to go now," said the boy, suddenly. "They're calling me."

"Who calls?" asked Olav Kirsten cupping a hand to his ear and looking down the street. "I hear nothing."

"Sometimes they worry. They cry out to me. They want me to come back to them. I must go." The boy stepped off the gate and paused. "Can I come and see you tomorrow? And Brian?" he added.

"Ja, Peter. You come tomorrow. I will show you things. Many things."

Olav Kirsten moved forward to lean on the gate and watch the boy run off down Allison Terrace. But he was gone. Instead he saw only Hone coming home from school.

"You see Peter, Hone?" he asked when his young neighbour reached the gate.

Hone stopped.

"Who's Peter?" he said.

"Peter's a boy. Young boy. Younger than you — much younger — but he knows you. He was here. He ran down the street."

"Didn't see any boy running down the street, Olav."

Brian, who had also come forward to the gate, whimpered quietly. Olav Kirsten bent and scratched his old dog's head.

"Is funny thing, Brian," he said. "He runs very fast I think."

Hone was puzzled. He was sure nobody had passed him going down Allison Terrace. He turned around and looked back down the street. Nothing.

"Sorry, Olav," he said.

Then he hitched up his school pack and passed on to the next house at the end of the garden wall.

The old man, though, stayed at the gate; before he went back to his digging, on that hot February afternoon so long ago, he shaded his eyes with his hand and looked down the street again. Nothing. But the boy had said he would be back the next day and the old man was glad.

"He will come tomorrow, Brian," he said to his dog.

Chapter 2.

The sun was setting when Olav Kirsten stopped working in his garden. Now, in the cool of the evening, he sat on his chair beside the cottage door with his evening meal on a tray. Brian sat at his feet with a bone that Mrs Wihongi — Hone's mother — had given him.

"A dog needs meat, Olav," she said. "It's only natural."

Before he ate his own meal Olav Kirsten thought about his food; he had grown it all from seed. I had to do some hard work, he thought, but now I have a fair reward.

"Perhaps Mrs Wihongi is right, Brian," he said to the dog. "Not to blame that you need meat. You are looking skinny. I give you sometimes meat more."

It was dark by the time he finished his meal. He went inside to fire the lamp that was his only source of night light. Inside, the little stone house was neat and clean and snug. At one end was a small cast-iron fireplace on a scoria hearth. To one side of the fireplace was a cupboard where he stored his wood and coal, and, to the other, a bookcase of old books in the Norwegian language. Between the bookcase and the door, which was in the middle of the front wall, was one of two windows and it was under this window that Olav Kirsten had his little kitchen: a sink and a spirit cooker and, under the bench, room for the few pots and dishes he needed.

At the other end of the house, the end opposite the fireplace, was his narrow bed beside which were two shipping trunks one of which contained the old man's few clothes. The other, standing on its end under the other window, served as a bedside table upon which stood a brass marine chronometer that ticked off the passing years and, nearer the bed, two framed photographs. One, in a dark wooden frame, was a family portrait taken when Olav Kirsten was a boy of about fifteen. He was sitting on the ground in front of a stone house, with his legs crossed, in front of his father, his mother, and his three older sisters. The picture was brown and silvered with age, reminding the old man that he came not only from a distant country but also from a distant time; another century. The other photo, smaller and more recent, was of Brian: a close-up of the dog's head and shoulders taken when he was young. Olav Kirsten had found a brown tin frame for the photo and the two pictures stood together on the trunk beside his bed.

But for a soft and comfortable armchair, the only other furniture comprised the wooden chair, which served its purpose both inside and out, and a small round table standing in the centre of the room. The table had a faded and limp woven cloth for a cover, a cloth that Olav Kirsten's mother had given to him before his first voyage. She had received it as a wedding gift from the Lapps of her village.

It was into this scene that the old man entered to sit in the armchair, with the lamp on the table behind his head, to read from the old books. At last, as his head nodded with sleepiness, he blew out the lamp and lay on his back in the narrow cot. He thought, for a moment, of the boy he had met that day and whom he hoped he would see again. Then he fell asleep for the rest of the night as he had done more than thirty-two thousand times before. On the floor rug beside his bed Brian waited in the dark until he was sure the old man was asleep. Only then did the old dog close his eyes and lay his grey jaw on the rug to sleep. And somewhere, far away to the north, a small boy, who had not yet seen four thousand nights, lay in dull but constant pain. With open and sometimes tearful eyes staring into the night he thought about the gentle, kind old man and his dog who were his new friends.

Meanwhile, next door, Hone Wihongi was in his bedroom doing his homework while his mother was in the living room watching television. Sometimes Hone leaned across from his chair, pulling the curtain aside to peer into the night. When the yellow glow faded from his neighbour's window he called out to his mother.

"Olav's light's out, mum."

"Okay, dear," called Mrs Wihongi, relieved that the old man, who had bought his land from her husband's family and had lived in his cottage since before she was born, was asleep in his bed, safe for another night.

She knew nothing of the meeting — between boy and old man — which had taken place earlier that day. Nor did she know of another meeting that day between two people discussing their special plans for Olav Kirsten's garden. And even if she had known of either meeting she could never have guessed how, together, they were going to change the lives of so many people in the quiet Mount Eden neighbourhood that she, Hone and Olav Kirsten had called home for so long.

Chapter 3.

Earlier that afternoon, as Hone was talking to Olav Kirsten about the boy he had called Peter, his friend Betty Grey, who had finished school the previous year, was working at her desk in a downtown office building not far away. It was her first job — she was the receptionist-typist for the small firm — and she was anxious to succeed. She found the work easy enough, and was receiving good training, although one of the partners always made her nervous.

Because she sat at the reception desk, at the only entrance to the firm's office, every person arriving or leaving had to pass her desk. Thus she was puzzled and alarmed when she thought she saw a small brown face — the face of young boy — watching her from behind the darkly-tinted glass door that led from the reception area, where she sat, to the firm's office suite beyond. How, she wondered, could he be there without her knowledge?

And was he beckoning to her? Did he want her to follow him? But where? And why?

Betty was puzzled and worried. No one should be in that corridor. She knew she would be in trouble if the boy were seen by the partners. But she was uncertain. Had she *really* seen something? Someone? Someone beckoning?

Could she see anything at all through the tinted glass?

She squinted. Stared hard at the door. There was no one there. But she had to be sure. So she left her desk and went through the door in time to see a small figure turning the corner at the end of the corridor where the partners shared a large office. She ran down the hall and around the corner but: nothing. She looked in the little kitchen, the only other room, but the boy — if it was a boy — had disappeared.

As she stood alone in the corridor, puzzled, thinking she must have imagined seeing someone, or something, she heard raised voices coming from the partners' office. It seemed that her employers were having an argument. The door was closed so she didn't hear everything but what she did hear frightened her.

She stopped, the mysterious boy forgotten, and listened. She couldn't help it.

"It's bullshit!" shouted an angry Michael Pike.

He was sitting at his office desk in front of a window. Behind him the Waitemata harbour sparkled in the late morning sun. But he didn't see the view. He was watching his partner, Wally Greensborough, who was standing across the desk from him.

"Come on, Wal," he continued, pleading now. "There's a couple of acres of prime real estate there, waiting. If we don't get it someone else will. Surely you can see that?"

15

"I told you," said his partner, trying to remain calm. "I've tried and tried."

"And?"

"Same story yesterday. He's a nice old joker. He listens to me politely. He shakes his head." Wally Greensborough shrugged. "He won't even discuss it."

"Shit!" said the irate Pike, thumping the desk with frustration.

He stood up and walked angrily to the other side of the large office from where he could see, distant from the city, the great rising of Mount Eden. And all around he could see many of the buildings from which he and Wally Greensborough had made their money. They had prospered, he reflected, because of the successful combination of his financial skills — some would say cunning — and the salesmanship of his partner. But now there was this Mount Eden business. He was puzzled not only by his partner's failure to convince the old man to sell but also by his distinct lack of enthusiasm for the entire project.

Composed now, he returned to his chair to face Greensborough again.

"Now then, Wal," he said quietly, patiently, to his partner who had, by this time, resumed his seat. "Let's go over it again, okay?"

"Yeah. Okay," said Greensborough, sounding resigned, impatient and annoyed.

"Right," continued Pike putting his hands together as if in prayer. "Now. Here's this old man, a hundred and fifty years old, right?"

"He's eighty something," said Greensborough. "More like ninety I think. I don't know exactly."

"Okay," said Pike shrugging. "What's it matter. He's old."

"Yeah. He's old alright. But he's not sick. And he's not stupid."

"Never mind about that. We'll come to that later," said Pike. "Now this old man, eighty? ninety? whatever, owns a couple of acres of dirt right in the middle of Mount Eden, a very desirable residential area, you must agree. A lovely bit of land sloping ever so gently to the sun. Right so far, Wal?"

"Yeah, but—"

"Now wait on, mate. Now this old joker, what's his name again, Wal?"

"Kirsten. Olav Kirsten. He's Norwegian or something."

At the mention of Olav Kirsten's name Betty moved closer to the closed door. She was nervous, afraid of being caught there, but she knew something important was going on. She felt she just *had* to keep listening.

"Yeah. Kirsten," Betty heard Pike say. "He gets this land when? — turn of the century or something — gets it for a bloody song. A few bucks, right?"

"It would have been a lot of money then," said Greensborough. "His life savings."

"Yeah," said Pike, frustrated. "But compared with now, not much, eh?

"Now," Pike continued, "Mr Wally Greensborough, the nicest salesman in the world, the joker who can talk anybody into anything with his charm and his smile, goes along to this old Mr Kirsten with a very fine offer. It *is* a very fine offer, indeed, isn't it, Wal?"

"Well, under normal circumstances it is a fine offer, Mike. We both know that. But these are not normal circumstances. And there's nothing normal about Mr Kirsten."

Pike got up and leaned across the desk to bring his face close to his partner's.

"Bullshit!" he said again.

"Come on, Mike," said Greensborough, annoyed with his partner's unusual obsession with this project.

"I mean it," said Pike again as he leaned back in his chair and clasped his hands behind his head. "We offer the old guy more money than he's ever seen in his life and guarantee him a brand new luxury apartment for the rest of his days. Come on, Wal, that's what I'd call a very fine offer under any circumstance."

"Except this one," insisted Greensborough. "For God's sake, man, *he* doesn't want a luxury apartment. He doesn't want anything. It doesn't matter what we say or do, or how much money we offer, he won't budge."

"Come on, Wal. He's human isn't he?"

"I don't know—" said Greensborough; Pike looked at him strangely. "—I mean of course he's human," he added. "But he's a strange old guy. Sort of a local legend."

18

Betty shook her head slowly and sadly. It's true, she thought. Mr Kirsten is a local legend.

"Oh, come on," said Pike. "Look. Let's keep going. See if I've got it all."

"Okay," said Greensborough.

"Right. Now the old man hasn't got any money. He owes the council for years and years of rates on the understanding that when he dies the council takes the land in payment. Right? The council can then sell the land to anyone."

"Yeah," said Greensborough. They had been through this many times. In those days Mount Eden was an independent borough with its own council; it hadn't been hard for Greensborough to find out about this unusual arrangement about the rates.

"And if we get the land we have to pay the back rates. That's all the council cares about?"

"Yeah," said Greensborough with a sigh.

"The council doesn't want the land?"

"No. They said they'd auction it."

"So anyone could get it, right?"

"Right."

"There are no other strings?"

"No."

"And we can put up a block of flats? It's big enough for planning and all that? The council will let us?"

"Right. Mike, we've been through all this before."

"I know. I know. But come on, Wal. Can't you see? It's the chance of a lifetime. Easier to deal with the old man now, and take care of him for a couple of years, than wait till he's gone and have to get in an auction with a million other greedy bastards. There's a fortune to be made out of that land. You must be able to see all that."

"Of course I can see it. But you've got to understand: I *can't* get through to the old man. He will *not* sell. To us or anyone. It's *impossible*."

"Nothing's impossible, Wal. You know that." Pike was insistent. "You're the best salesman in the country. You're half the reason for our success. We're an amazing team."

He picked up a thick file and waved it in the air.

"Look. I've done my bit. All the contracts. All the plans and specifications. Titles. Finance. The bank's right behind us now, you know that. Cash flow. It's all here, Wal." He dumped the file heavily on the desk. "All we need is the old man's agreement and now you say it's impossible."

"Well it is," said Greensborough angrily.

Betty could tell, from the sound of his voice, that Wally Greensborough was moving towards the door and was about to come into the corridor so she hurried back to her desk. Greensborough opened the door and stood there, holding the door handle, talking back into the office to his partner.

"Why don't you go out there yourself," Betty heard him say. "Go and talk to him. You'll see."

She picked up typing where she had left off.

"I bloody might," she heard Pike shout down the corridor. "I just bloody might."

The door slammed and Greensborough left the building without even glancing at her. That was unusual; he was usually kind and polite. But he was obviously angry and, although she didn't understand everything that was said between him and Mr Pike, she knew that something was going on, that Mr Greensborough didn't like it, and that whatever it was it was bad news for Mr Kirsten.

She stopped working and went down the corridor again hoping she might find the mysterious boy. But there was no one there. She looked at the closed door of the partners' office and wondered what she should do. She knew she wasn't allowed to talk about anything that went on in the firm, including business discussions between the partners, but she decided that because of Mr Kirsten, and because his land once belonged to the Wihongi family, she should probably tell her friend Hone.

Chapter 4.

The boy returned to the garden the next day as he had said he would. It was late in the afternoon; the old man had stopped his work when he sensed the boy standing silently behind him. Now they were crouching in the middle path of the garden with Brian lying between them.

"See, Peter. These are the beans. They grow strong and big. And when I talk with them is good. Kind words they like. They are happy and grow good.

"Lettuce," he said, pointing to a small plot crowded with plants.

"Do you talk to the lettuce?" asked the boy.

"Not talk. Touch. Lettuce like touch like this." And the old man gently fondled the pale and loosely formed young plants.

"You do," he said to the boy while concentrating on the lettuce. "But nice. You must feel nice in here," and he patted his chest lightly with his other hand.

"In here?" asked the boy, patting his own chest in imitation of the old man.

"Ja. Ja. Feel nice to plants *inside*. Is important."

The boy sat on the dirt path and touched the lettuce as he had been shown.

22

"Feels nice," he said, smiling.

"Some of the plants like to be spoken to gently," explained the old man. "And some need stronger words. Like naughty boys," he added, chuckling to himself.

The boy laughed, too.

The old man enjoyed showing him the vegetables and flowers. He explained that summer was nearly over, that different plants would grow in the winter, and that it was his job to have everything ready for planting at the right time. He showed the boy the bees at work, lifting one out of a yellow dahlia and cradling it in his hands to show the sacs of pollen on the insect's legs, and the hairy little body designed to ensure the survival of the plant species.

"Not sting us," he said as the boy watched the bee crawling restlessly around his palm, its feelers waving frantically ahead. "Not sting us if we have kind hands. You try, Peter." And he placed the tiny creature in the boy's cupped hands.

Together, with Brian at their side, they lifted the wooden lid of the compost, moving their faces through the sickly sweet warmth that rose to caress them. Then the old man scooped up a handful of the new earth.

"Is all dead and rubbish and not good one day," he said. "But now is good."

He lifted out some worms and dangled them over his fingers. He explained the worms' work — digesting and breaking down the rotting vegetation and creating tunnels for ventilation —

and showed the boy how long and fat they could get in the richness of the compost. And, in the far corner of the land, the boy watched quietly as the old man lay flat on the dirt beside a square of uncultivated ground, rank with weeds, and stretched his arm into the growth. When he withdrew his arm, only moments later, it was covered with insects: beetles and bugs and spiders, insects by the hundred. His leathery skin could hardly be seen.

"Insects," said the man to the boy. "Is the creatures of the past and the future. They are our friends, too. And they all have their jobs to do."

"Is this where they live?" asked the boy.

Olav Kirsten stood up, shaking the insects off his hand and arm, back into the patch of weeds.

"Everywhere insects live," he said. "And weeds, too. But this is a special place I keep just for them."

"People don't like insects and weeds."

The old man shrugged. "Nothing can help it the shape of its life," he said. "I tell you a special secret, Peter." And he leaned down and lowered his voice. "Sometimes I think insects are better people than people. And weeds are better still. Much better. Because they hurt nobody or nothing."

"Yes," said the boy, looking up at him. "I know."

The old man straightened quickly, surprised.

"Perhaps I tell you things too big," he said, stroking his beard thoughtfully. "Never mind, Peter. We shall drink."

Brian, lying at the old man's feet, lifted himself and pushed past them both to stand panting at the dented tin dish lying empty at the cottage door. The boy filled the dish from the barrel at the corner of the cottage, as the old man had shown him, and put it down for the dog who stood over it, slurping noisily at the cool rain water.

Once inside the cottage the boy was entranced by the two photographs he found standing on the trunk. He knew that, to the old man, each photo was a treasure. He knew that the real value of such treasures lies in the memories they represent, and that one's memories can never be shared. He knew that, compared with the old man, he had very few memories but that those he had were more precious than possessions because they could never be lost or stolen.

Meanwhile the old man poured two glasses of water from a big bottle and set them on the table. When the boy turned around the old man was sitting quietly, his eyes closed. The boy pressed the old man's shoulder softly.

"What are you doing?" he asked quietly. "Are you sick?"

The old man opened his eyes and smiled.

"Not sick, Peter," he said cheerfully. "Drink. Drink," he urged waving his hand towards the glasses of water. "Is rain water. Very sweet. Very good."

"No thank you," said the boy.

"What were you doing?" he asked when the old man finished drinking. "Why did you close your eyes and sit so still. I thought you were sick. I don't want you to be sick. It's awful to be sick."

"Not sick. I was thinking of the water."

"Were you?" asked the boy, curiously.

"Water is good. And pure. Part of the Big Life, Peter."

"What Big Life?" asked the boy.

"Everything—" the old man held out his arms as if to embrace the whole world. "—is part of Big Life," he said. "Everything."

"Am I part of the Big Life?"

"Ja. Everything. Everyone. Big Life is everywhere. Even in the wood." He knocked the table with his knuckles.

"What does it mean: the Big Life?"

The old man looked at the boy, thinking, before answering. Then he said: "Is my words, Peter. My English words. I talk too much. You shouldn't listen to an old man."

He brushed aside the boy's questioning.

"People don't like my talk," he said. "They think: crazy old man. Don't like."

"I like your talk, Mr Kirsten," said the boy, sincerely.

"How do you know my name?"

"Everyone knows your name," replied the boy. "Everyone. Auntie said."

The old man relaxed. "Well you should call me Olav, Peter," he said. "Olav. Is a good old name."

The boy nodded. "I've got to go now, Olav," he said suddenly.

"Are you going home?"

"My mother is calling to my father. She is crying with worry. She thinks I've gone away. Can't you hear?" said the boy, standing at the door.

"No," said Olav Kirsten. "Don't hear good."

"Oh, yes," said the boy at the door. "Well thank you, Olav," he said over his shoulder. And then he was gone.

Chapter 5.

Early that morning, in the offices of Greensborough and Pike, Betty Grey was speaking nervously to Wally Greensborough who was standing beside her desk.

"It's just that I couldn't help overhearing what you and Mr Pike were talking about yesterday; you know, the Mount Eden project."

Greensborough nodded. He was interested in what the girl had to say.

"Well, I live in Mount Eden and I know Mr Kirsten. Not to talk to or anything, it's just that, well, *everyone* knows Mr Kirsten. He's a real identity in Mount Eden. You can't push him out, Mr Greensborough, you can't. It wouldn't be right."

"I know, Betty," said Greensborough quietly.

"But what about Mr Pike?"

"Maybe he'll find a way." Greensborough shrugged. "I don't know."

"Well I hope he doesn't," said Betty. "Everyone likes Mr Kirsten and his garden. And he gives it all away, you know. All the stuff he grows. It's good, too. He doesn't use sprays or anything like that. It's all natural."

"I know, Betty. I've been there don't forget. I like the old bloke, too."

"Well I hope that nothing happens to him, that's all. He should be left alone."

Betty Grey felt, and looked, embarrassed. She hadn't meant to be quite so outspoken.

"Mr Greensborough," she added nervously. "You won't tell Mr Pike what I said will you? I don't think he'd like it."

Greensborough smiled kindly and shook his head. "I don't think he'd like it either," he said. "So I won't tell him."

Betty was relieved. She knew she could trust him, just as she knew she could *not* trust his partner, Michael Pike. And she knew it was time to tell Hone what was happening.

It was a long walk from the bus stop, along Mount Eden Road, past Edenside High School, and up to the top of Allison Terrace, so Betty stopped at the school gates. Standing beneath the twisted old pohutukawas, which hung over the footpath, littering it with their brittle grey-green leaves, she could see, across the asphalt playgrounds, the cream-painted red-roofed buildings of the old school. It was her old school where her friend Hone Wihongi was now a senior student.

It's a lovely school, she thought. And Mount Eden is such a nice place to grow up.

She walked on, listening to the rhythmic scratching and clicking of the cicadas that reminded her, even more, of her summery schooldays. At the turn into Allison Terrace she stopped again and looked up the street to the very end where Hone's was the last house before the entrance to the mountain park.

She remembered, when they were children, walking with Hone and their primary school class to the top of the mountain and scrambling down into the deep crater. And although the mountain had been their playground since childhood — as familiar to her and Hone as their own back yards — she was still moved and thrilled by Mr Kirsten's talk to the class. Standing at the rim of the crater he had explained how important the mountain had been to the Maori people of the past. He showed them the weather-beaten shapes and outlines that had once been garden terraces and food-storage pits, whare — the houses — where the people had lived, even the great meeting house, te whare whakairo, helping them to visualise the pa that had once been there.

And she remembered, later, at high school, when she and Hone used to take the younger classes into Mr Kirsten's garden, how the old man would show the children many of the historic things he had found there, and explain to them how interesting and exciting a place Mount Eden had once been and how it was possible to live close to nature in this historic, busy and modern neighbourhood so close to the city.

She walked on then, without stopping, until she reached the walled garden. She could see the old man, close to his cottage, crouching down, apparently talking to himself.

He talks to the plants, she reminded herself. She watched quietly, sadly, for a moment before moving on.

"Hullo, Betty," said Mrs Wihongi with a smile. Then she noticed Betty's worried look. "What's the matter, dear?"

"Oh, Mrs Wihongi," said the girl. "I've got to tell Hone something. Is he home?"

"No, dear. I think he's still at school. Playing touch I think." She looked at her watch. "He won't be home for a while yet."

"Can I tell you, Mrs Wihongi, so you can tell Hone? But you mustn't tell anyone else."

"Of course, Betty. Come in."

Mrs Wihongi was a jolly woman with a large round face topped with thick, wavy, black hair streaked with grey. She had fat sides and heavy breasts that heaved violently when she laughed. But she didn't laugh as she sat in the living room and listened to Betty's story.

"Now, what on earth's the matter, dear?" asked Mrs Wihongi.

"Well," said Betty. "I found out that one of the people at my work—"

"Ye-es," said Mrs Wihongi patiently. Hone had told her that Betty had been thrilled to get the job with Greensborough and Pike, one of the biggest property developers in town, and she was disappointed to hear that something might be going wrong.

"Well, they — that is, Mr Pike — he's trying to buy Mr Kirsten's land," said Betty.

"What?" Mrs Wihongi was astonished.

"Yes. They want to put up a big block of flats."

Mrs Wihongi was shocked. She put a hand to her mouth.

"They want to get rid of him," continued Betty. "I think they'll do anything to get his land. Anything. Especially Mr Pike."

Mrs Wihongi, her hand still at her mouth, shook her head gravely and slowly. Then she sat back in her chair, thinking.

"Who else knows about this, Betty?" she asked, taking her hand away from her mouth.

"Nobody. Well not as far as I know. No one outside the office anyway. I only know about it by accident. I heard them arguing. But I'm not supposed to talk about anything that happens at the office. I'll get into real trouble if they find out I told you."

"Don't worry, dear. I won't tell anyone."

Betty Grey looked and felt relieved.

"Anyway, I've seen a man at Olav's a few times," continued Mrs Wihongi. "That must be your Mr Pike."

"No. That'll be Mr Greensborough," said Betty. "He's nice. He likes Mr Kirsten. He doesn't want to hurt him. He won't be back, I'm sure."

"And Pike? The other one?"

"Oh, Mrs Wihongi, he's horrible. He and Mr Greensborough had a big argument. I think he might try to talk to Mr Kirsten himself. But he's horrible. I don't like him at all."

"But Olav won't sell. I *know* he won't," said Mrs Wihongi firmly.

"But they're such a big firm. They've got so much money," said the girl, sounding afraid. "And Mr Pike's ruthless. He's got a reputation for it."

"But they can't *make* him sell, Betty."

"They might. Mr Pike would do anything. Truly, Mrs Wihongi, I wouldn't trust him a bit."

"Don't worry, dear," said Mrs Wihongi, sounding more confident than she felt. "I'll tell Hone when he gets home. But we won't tell anyone else. It's our secret for the moment and I'll find out from Olav what's going on. He'll tell me. I'll find out, don't you worry."

But Doris Wihongi had an awful feeling that things were going wrong for her old neighbour and that nothing she could say or do would make a difference. She wished Hone were home. Perhaps he'd know what to do.

Betty Grey, too, sensed that something unpleasant was going to happen soon. And certain that she wanted nothing to do with it — whatever it was — she decided it was time to leave her job at Greensborough and Pike.

Chapter 6.

The next day, just before lunch, Olav Kirsten was walking down the middle path with Hone who, at the principal's request, had slipped away from school to organise another class visit to the old man's garden. He had made the arrangements and was about to leave when he saw a Rolls Royce parked on the street. He could see a man — he assumed it was Greensborough or Pike — sitting alone in the front.

"Olav. Who's that in the flash car?"

Olav squinted. The sun reflecting off the car didn't make it easy for his old eyes.

He shrugged. "Don't know," he said.

"Well, whoever it is they're waiting for me to go. They want to talk to you." His mother and Betty had told him about the developers' plans for the old man's garden and he didn't like the look of the visitor. "You be careful, Olav," he added. "Be careful, eh."

"Ja," said the old man.

"Anyway, I've got to get back to school now. I'll see you tomorrow with the third formers."

"Ja. Tomorrow," said Olav Kirsten, walking the last few steps to the gate with his young friend and neighbour.

"Hone?" He spoke when they were at the gate. The young man waited. "Will Peter come tomorrow?"

"Who's Peter?"

"Peter is Peter. Is at your school I think. He said your name."

"Lots of Peters, Olav. Why?"

The old man shrugged. "Is my friend. Nice boy."

"I don't know," said Hone truthfully. "What's his other name?"

The old man shrugged again. "Just Peter. Other name I don't know. Don't worry. Goodbye, Hone."

"Goodbye, Olav. Tomorrow, eh."

It was only when Hone was well down Allison Terrace, on his way back to school, that Michael Pike got out of the car. Olav saw him, and went to the gate, shading his eyes against the glare.

"Mr Kirsten?" enquired Pike cheerfully.

"Ja?" the old man said, politely, to the stranger.

"G'day," said Pike extending his hand. "I'm Michael Pike."

Olav Kirsten took the hand but knew at once he didn't like this man.

"Is not for me, a big flat," he said to Pike as he had said to Greensborough.

They were in the cottage now.

"Look," he said, gesturing outside. "This I like. My plants. Here I want to be. My house. Here I want to die. On my land. And then—" he shrugged his shoulders to say he didn't care what happened once he was gone.

That gave Pike an idea.

"Well, listen, Mr Kirsten," he said quickly. "What about we buy the land now and let you live here, you know, until you're, well, gone, you know what I mean. I promise we won't do anything until then. How about that? You can have all the money now, go for a world trip or something. You'd be rich."

"No money. Don't want rich," Olav Kirsten insisted. He was sorry he had invited Pike inside. "Nothing I want except stay here. On my land. Is all. Nothing else. Go please, Mr Pike."

Brian, who had been restless during Pike's visit, stood with his master at the cottage door and watched with the old man as Pike turned his car towards town.

"Is not a nice man, Brian," Olav said to the dog. And, to his surprise, and as far as he knew for the first time in the dog's life, a dark growl rumbled deep in the old dog's chest.

Doris Wihongi, too, was watching as Pike's Rolls Royce turned and headed back down Allison Terrace. When it was gone she went directly to the phone in the hall.

"That'll be him, Mrs Park," Betty Grey said in a whisper. "That'll be him alright. They had another terrible row this morning. I think Mr Greensborough wants them to drop the whole

36

thing but Mr Pike won't. They were really angry at each other. You could hear the argument all over the office.

"Anyway, listen, Mrs Park," she continued. "I don't like it here and I'm leaving. I told Mr Greensborough this morning."

"You quit?"

"Yes. One week."

"Probably just as well, dear," said Mrs Wihongi. She was glad Betty was leaving a job she didn't like but was aware that without Betty they wouldn't know what Greensborough and Pike were up to.

And when Hone got home from school she told him what Betty had said.

"I was there," said Hone. "I thought it must have been Pike. I thought he looked quite mean and ugly and unpleasant."

"Oh, Hone, what are we going to do about it? Poor Olav."

"Don't worry, mum," said Hone, glad that he was now old enough to make decisions and take charge. "I have to take a third form class to Olav's tomorrow morning. I won't be able to do much, not right away, but I'll ask him about it then. I'll ask him outright what's going on."

"I'm going to ask him about it tomorrow, too," said Mrs Wihongi.

"Good," said Hone. "We'll both ask him and compare notes when I get home."

"Oh, yes, Hone," said Mrs Wihongi with relief. Suddenly her son seemed so tall and broad and strong and handsome. And so confident.

"And, mum."

"Yes, Hone."

"Don't worry. Everything will be fine."

"Oh, Hone," said Mrs Wihongi proudly. "You seem so grown up. You remind me so much of your father."

And that made Hone feel especially proud.

Chapter 7.

The morning was fine and clear so the thirteen-year-olds in Hone's charge were glad to be out of the classroom and in Olav Kirsten's garden. Hone listened as the old man talked to the children, explaining how plants grow using food and water from the soil and energy from the sun. His explanations were simple and quaint but his appearance, his accent, and his gentleness fascinated the children so they listened carefully, taking notes. They followed up and down the paths as he walked about showing them his vegetables and flowers, his herb garden, his small orchard of ripening apples and pears, his grapes and passion fruit, his compost, his beehive, the garden full of insects where the weeds were allowed to grow, and the pond.

Finally he took them into the shade of the old trees, pine and *macrocarpa* mixed with puriri, rata and kauri, growing closely together in one corner.

"This is where the birds live," he whispered.

By standing together quietly, and waiting patiently, the children saw the friendly little piwakawaka, a handsome tui dressed in his finest tuxedo who gave them an elaborate flute recital, and a pair of plump and comely kereru, dressed in shimmering green and rich cream.

There were even two curious and mischievous weka who made the children laugh as they stepped boldly in front of them across the springy floor of Olav Kirsten's shady little forest. And the old man showed them the more numerous immigrants including blackbirds, thrushes, starlings, mynas, finches, silver-eyes and common sparrows who shared their urban home with the native birds of the Aotearoa bush.

When the talk was over, and the children were wandering around the garden on their own, Hone stood quietly with the old man, watching them. He knew from experience that meeting Olav Kirsten was a lesson in itself. The children could sense the old man's love of his land and his plants, and to be allowed to explore his large garden was an experience most of them would remember for the rest of their lives.

But Hone wanted to ask his neighbour and friend about the strangers trying to buy his land; he was trying to find just the right words when the old man interrupted his thoughts.

"Is no Peter," Olav Kirsten said. "Where is Peter?"

"There are lots of Peters, Olav," said Hone. "I don't know which one you mean."

"Is a boy. In your school I think. He knows you, Hone. He said your name to me."

"Is he here? Do you see him here?" asked Hone. "Is it him?" he asked, pointing to a fair-headed boy who was sitting on the path, drawing in his book. "His name is Peter."

"No, no, Hone," Olav said. "Is one of your people. A Maori boy."

"A Maori boy?" Hone was surprised. He couldn't think of any Maori boys at school, of any age, named Peter.

"Ja. A Maori boy. This big." Olav used the side of his hand to mark the boy's height against his own body.

"What's his other name?"

The old man shrugged. "Don't know. Just Peter."

"Maybe he goes to the Brothers," said Hone, puzzled.

"Not Brothers," said the old man positively. "I know Brothers' uniform. He is at your school. He knows you, Hone."

"Well, I don't know any Maori boys called Peter at Edenside, Olav. Honest. How do you know him anyway?"

"He comes to me sometimes," said the old man. "He is quiet. Very unusual child I can tell. He understands me and my plants. He listens. And he looks at me so clever."

As Hone watched the old man turned to stare out beyond the wall, stroking his beard, as if looking for something. Or someone. Suddenly, recovering himself, he added: "You'll see some time, Hone. You'll see. A special boy. And a friend of Brian."

Hone nodded. The old man seemed preoccupied. He wasn't sure now if it was a good time to talk to him about the property

41

developers. But he had promised his mother that he would.

"Olav?"

"Ja?"

"Who came to see you yesterday in the big car?"

"Arrhh," grumped the old man, obviously irritated. Hone had never seen his friend angry or annoyed.

"Who was it?" he asked again. "Is he bothering you?"

"Is nothing," said the old man. "A foolish and greedy man. Is no problem. I told him."

"Told him what?"

The old man turned and looked directly at the young man. He spoke slowly and seriously.

"He wants to give me money, Hone. Lots of money. He wants to buy all this." He opened his arms to embrace the whole garden.

"He wants your land? Is that it, Olav? He wants to buy your land?"

"Ja. Land. Land. Buy, buy, buy. Money, money, money. Already I told the other one."

"What other one?" Hone didn't want to get his old friend upset but he needed to know what was going on.

"Other one comes. He's okay. Okay. Nice man. A good man, I think. One of your people, Hone. Peter's people."

"Peter's people?"

42

"Yes. A Maori man. Or — you know — part Maori. Little bit. I can tell. I told him, Hone, I won't sell. He comes back sometimes. I always tell him the same. No sell. He understands I think."

"But the other man? The man yesterday? What about him?"

"Is not a nice man, Hone. A bad man. I know in here—" he tapped the side of his head, "—and here," he tapped over his heart.

"Well, what did he say? Exactly? It could be important, Olav."

"Don't remember. Is not important. I told him go away. No sell. No money. Go away. Is all."

Hone nodded slowly. He thought the old man sounded tired. He decided to ask no more questions; to wait, instead, until he had time to compare notes with his mother. She, too, had planned to speak to the old man later in the day.

Meanwhile he had to get the third-formers back to school for lunch. As they lined up in the middle path a girl, who had been elected by the class, stepped forward to thank Mr Kirsten for talking to them and letting them see his garden. As she spoke, and as the children shuffled in their places waiting impatiently for her to finish, a small brown face, unseen by anyone but Brian, watched from the cottage window.

Olav Kirsten walked with Hone and the third formers to the gate and then waited there, watching them straggle down Allison Terrace, until they were no more than a bobbing blur in the distance.

"Peter will come today, I think," he said. "I will ask him his name. I will ask him his school. Is funny Hone doesn't know him. Funny."

He was speaking to Brian. But Brian wasn't there.

Chapter 8.

Olav's thoughts about the boy, and then about the whereabouts of his dog, were interrupted by the sight of Mrs Wihongi bustling down the street. He waited for her at the gate.

"Ah, Mrs Wihongi," he called out cheerfully. "You want lunch? You are just in time. Come."

But Doris Wihongi wanted no lunch. She knew that Hone had just left and she hoped he had asked the old man about the visitor in the Rolls Royce. Now it was her turn. So she declined lunch and became businesslike.

"No, Olav," she said firmly. "I can't stop for lunch but I do want to talk about something."

The old man stopped and waited.

"Olav. What's going on with these people who want to buy your land?"

"How do you know about it? I didn't say it to you."

"Hone told me."

"But I only just now—" said the old man but Mrs Wihongi interrupted him.

"Now what's going on?" she asked firmly.

"Is nothing," said the old man. "I tell Hone. They want to buy my land, is all. Lots of money."

"And?"

"And what? What do you mean, Mrs Wihongi?"

"What did you say?"

"No. I say no of course. What do you think I say, Mrs Wihongi?"

"But they've been bothering you, haven't they? Coming around and bothering you? I know, Olav. I know."

"The first one I don't mind him. Is a nice man. He understands I think."

"That's Mr Greensborough. How many times has he been here?"

"Three. Maybe four. I'm not sure."

"And the other one? Mr Pike? The one who came yesterday in the big car?"

"Ah. Pike," was all the old man said.

Mrs Wihongi noticed, as Hone had, that the old man was preoccupied, staring down the street as if looking for someone.

"Olav," she said sharply, trying to regain his attention. "Look at me. You must tell me what's going on."

The old man turned and looked down again on Mrs Wihongi's kind but worried face.

"They're partners, Olav," she said. "The nice one and the bad one. They belong to the same firm — Greensborough and Pike — and they want your land. Don't you understand, Olav? They are not good people." She sighed with frustration. "Well what did Pike say?"

"Same thing, Mrs Wihongi. Always same. I sell. They buy. Lots of money for me. But I don't want their money, Mrs Wihongi," he said. "They should be understanding that and leave me alone."

"Olav," said Mrs Wihongi gently. "I don't think they will leave you alone. I don't think people like that stop until they get what they want no matter who they hurt."

She could see that the gentle old man was bothered by the affair. And his attention was drifting again. He kept looking down the street.

"Listen, Olav," she said loudly to make him listen. "You must tell me if anything else happens; if they come again. Olav, listen. You must tell me. Do you promise?"

The old man nodded obediently.

Not entirely satisfied by his response Mrs Wihongi bustled away home while the old man returned to his cottage to sit on his outside chair and eat his lunch.

Later in the afternoon he was working in his glasshouse. He had been unsettled by all the questions about the men trying to buy his land but he felt better when he sensed the boy at the door. He turned around.

"Ah, Peter, you come," he said as the boy stepped into the humid warmth of the glasshouse to watch him at work sowing spinach in seed trays.

"This spinach I grow for the mission," he said. "For the homeless people. Is good food, spinach. They like it."

When his work in the glasshouse was finished they walked up and down the garden rows talking to and touching the plants, with Brian padding along behind. And when it was time for the boy to leave Olav Kirsten walked with him to the gate and they stood there together.

"Olav," said the boy looking up to the old man. "Next time can we go inside and talk about the Big Life some more?"

Olav Kirsten laughed. "Is not much to say about the Big Life. Is what you feel inside. Your people know, Peter. You should ask your matua," The boy looked disappointed. "But if you want, we talk some more," he added.

The boy smiled now. He looked small and frail but his smile was broad.

"But, Peter," the old man added cautiously. "You are a good boy, a clever boy, but these are my ideas. Old man's ideas. Not everyone would like."

The boy smiled again. But this time it was a patient, indulgent smile. A smile that made the old man feel as though he, the boy — solemn and wise — was waiting for him, the old man, to learn and understand.

"Peter," said the old man suddenly, remembering. "Where do you go to school?"

"I don't go to school, Olav. I am sick too often for school."

"Sick?" The old man was puzzled. "But Hone? You know Hone Wihongi?"

"Oh, yes, Olav. I know Hone and his school. I went there once last year. But not now. Goodbye, Olav."

"Is good," said the old man. "And your name, Peter? What is it your name? I want to tell Hone your name."

But the boy was gone.

"He seemed to be talking to someone, Hone," said Mrs Wihongi, "I watched carefully but there was nobody there."

She and Hone were in the kitchen together with a cup of tea. Hone had just got home from school.

"He talks to the plants all the time," said Hone. "He was so busy talking to them — just now — he didn't even see me when I came past."

"But it looked more like he was talking to a person," said Mrs Wihongi. "A conversation, you know. But there was nobody there.

"Poor old soul," she added. "Maybe he's really getting past it, Hone." She used her first finger to point at her temple. "Maybe he should sell for his own good. Before it's too late."

"No way, mum," said Hone firmly. "He's perfectly fine. I was there this morning, remember. He was perfect. I think he's worried about these property developers. The whole thing seems to be getting him down. He really needs help."

His mother nodded but she didn't know what to do.

"By the way, mum," Hone asked. "Has he ever mentioned a boy to you? A boy called Peter?"

"No," said Mrs Wihongi. "Why?"

"Well have you seen a little boy in there with him over the last few days; a little Maori boy?"

"No, Hone. Not that I've noticed. And I think I notice just about everything that goes on in there you know. Why?"

"Oh, I don't know really," said Hone. "Something he said that's all. About a boy called Peter."

Then they talked about what Greensborough and Pike might do if they really wanted to push him out. But because they didn't know everything about the rates arrangement that the old man had with the council they couldn't understand how urgent the deal might seem to the developers. They ended the discussion with Hone promising to find out what he could about the property's planning arrangements, while his mother promised to keep an eye on their neighbour, making notes about any visitors he might have.

"Including a boy," said Hone. "About twelve I think. Maybe thirteen, I'm not sure."

"Yes, Hone. Including a boy. What's his name again?

"Peter."

"Yes. Peter. A boy called Peter."

Chapter 9.

Except for the occasional and welcome visits of the boy, the next couple of weeks passed quietly for Olav Kirsten. The two men, Greensborough and Pike, didn't visit him again so he supposed they had lost interest in his land.

But Hone and his mother were not so naïve. Mrs Wihongi kept a watch out for another visit by Pike, dashing to the window whenever she heard a car, while Hone asked Betty Grey to help by visiting the council's town planning office to find out what she could about Olav's property looking for anything that the developers could exploit. She had been properly trained to understand town planning, but had ended her job at Greensborough and Pike and was home for a couple of weeks until she started a new job.

Each afternoon, when Hone got home from school, the three of them had a meeting in the living room. On the fourth afternoon Betty had something important to report. She told them she had discovered, as Greensborough had before her, that the Mount Eden Borough Council had deferred its property rates on Olav's land on the understanding that when he sold the land he would repay all that was due, plus interest, from the great deal of money he would make from the sale.

"How did you find out that?" asked her mother.

"I had an idea, from what I heard Mr Pike say, and in the end the town clerk confirmed it," said Betty with a smile. "But, listen. There's more. If Mr Kirsten stays on the land until he dies the council will auction the land to recover all the rates."

Hone stood up suddenly.

"That's it!" he said, going to the window to look out at Olav's garden.

"That's what?"

"It's the clue we've been looking for," he said, turning around. "The reason Greensborough and Pike are in such a hurry."

Obviously, explained Hone, the land's unique position and size would push up the auction price. So the property developers would rather deal with Olav now — while he's alive — than face an auction later when they'd have to compete with all the other buyers.

No wonder Greensborough and Pike were the most successful property developers in the country: of all such developers only they had discovered the Mount Eden garden of Olav Kirsten.

"But they haven't been back, have they?" he said.

"No. He's had no visitors at all."

Hone was uneasy about that. Surely, he thought, Pike wouldn't give up so easily so he must be planning something.

52

"What about the boy?" Hone asked.

"What boy?" asked Betty.

"Oh, a mysterious boy that visits Olav. He talks about him all the time but no one's ever seen him."

"A little Maori boy?" asked Betty.

"Yes. Have you seen him?"

Betty felt a shiver at the back of her neck.

"Oh, no," she said quickly, still unsure of what she had seen. "I just wondered, that's all."

"So, mum?"

Hone's mother assured him that there had been no visits to Olav's by anyone. Man or boy. None at all.

But she was wrong.

Without her knowledge the boy had continued to call on the old man almost every afternoon in those days before Easter. He and Olav Kirsten had spent many hours together, more of them in the cottage than in the garden.

The boy asked the old man about the Big Life, and it was on this subject that they spent most of their time. The old man explained his belief that life was compelled to leave the Big Life and exist apart for its own sake in myriad earthly forms.

"People and dogs, fish and frogs, insects and birds, flowers and trees, are all little pieces of the Big Life," he said. "And all the little pieces die. And the dead pieces feed the living pieces."

"But trees and plants don't kill things to eat," said the boy.

"Life starts with the sun and the rain, Peter, and moves through all living things," said the old man. "It moves through the grass and leaves and fruit which some animals eat. It moves through those animals which are then eaten by others. Is true, Peter, that the kauri, anchored to the forest floor, does not hunt like lion. But, like lion, it gets life and strength from the dead animals and plants that went before it and now enrich the soil at its roots. Is all part of the Big Life, Peter. We all belong there where there is no beginning and no end."

And the boy understood because he had heard such things before from his tupuna.

During their talks the old man noticed that Brian would sit, listening, at the boy's feet as if he could understand what the child was thinking and saying. He thought he noticed too that, during the boy's visits, the plants seemed to grow a little extra, or turn a little greener or brighter. And when he couldn't find quite the right English word, slipping accidentally into the old language —Landsmål — the language of his village, he discovered that the boy understood him anyway.

The boy was fluent in the Maori language, too, so that they could talk in English and Maori. And that led the old man to question the boy about his family. What was his name? And where, exactly, did he live? And always, later, when the boy had gone, the old man would realise that none of his questions had been answered and that, in the end, he knew as little about the boy as he knew on that first day when he found him at the garden gate.

Finally he realised that no one — not even Mrs Wihongi, who was always calling in to see him about something — had ever met the boy. And he remembered the talk he had had with Hone. If anyone should have known the boy it was Hone.

"I don't know who he is or why he visits us," he said to Brian. "But it doesn't matter. He is a nice boy. A good boy."

Chapter 10.

Early on the Wednesday morning after Easter Mrs Wihongi saw the Rolls Royce arrive at her neighbour's gate. Watching alone from her window — Hone was at school — she saw the man she now knew was Michael Pike open the garden gate and walk slowly up the middle path to the door of the cottage. She knew Olav Kirsten wasn't in the cottage. She knew he was in the glasshouse and she assumed that Pike would find him there. Only minutes later, however, she saw Pike return slowly down the path, get into his car and drive away.

The old man had been in the glasshouse, just as Mrs Wihongi had known, but Pike hadn't bothered to look for him there. He had knocked only lightly on the cottage door as if hoping he wouldn't be heard. Busy in the glasshouse the old man didn't hear the knock. But Brian did and, growling quietly, slipped out of the glasshouse. His old master, working away at the bench, guessed from the dog's growl that Pike was in the garden but by the time he got to the front of the cottage the man and his car were gone. Puzzled, but otherwise unconcerned, the old man went back to his work.

During the next few hours, while Olav Kirsten worked in his glasshouse, the plants in the rows to each side of the middle path shrivelled and died. Thus, when he emerged from his glasshouse, ready for lunch, he was greeted by such a dreadful scene that he slumped down into his chair, his old heart banging with shock, and stared in disbelief at the remains of his beautiful garden.

The two neat rows of vegetables — gardens that had been tall, green, healthy and lush — were each reduced to an ugly line of limp and tangled leaves and stalks, entirely without life. And when he looked more closely, when he could bear to stand from his chair and walk the length of the path, he saw that even the insects were dead: grasshoppers and katydids, mantises and spiders, even the caterpillars, moths, butterflies, slugs and snails which he tolerated, were all lying dead in the foul remains of his once pure garden. Not knowing what to do, unable to move, the old man stood shocked, quiet and still, with Brian at his side, for some minutes.

"Someone bad has come," he said to Brian at last. "That man Pike I think. You knew, Brian. You growled. Is not nice that he do this. Not nice."

And he returned to his chair, without appetite. He was still there in the afternoon when the boy appeared. They didn't speak but, as they surveyed the awful destruction, the old man knew that the boy shared his pain. There was a sense, too, of anger, and it moved between them.

'It was that man, Pike,' thought the boy and the boy's thought touched the man.

"How do you know it about the man Pike?" asked Olav Kirsten.

"What?" said the boy, turning around, surprised.

"Pike? You know him, Peter. How you know him?"

"You heard me, Olav. You heard me," said the boy.

"Of course I heard you. Yes," said the old man, looking, with sad eyes, at the boy.

'But I didn't speak,' thought the boy.

"How do you do this thing, Peter? You frighten me. How do you do it to speak and not to move your mouth?"

'It is not new,' thought the boy to the man. *'What is new, my old friend, is that in your sadness you can hear me.'*

'You are a strange and wonderful mystery, Peter,' thought the old man. *'I do not know why you come to me.'*

'There is no mystery in the Big Life, Olav. I come when I can because you and Brian are my friends. But, Olav, you must watch for that evil man. He is possessed by his greed for money. You must be prepared to defend yourself against him.'

'How? How can I defend myself against such bad things?'

'It may take violence to defend yourself against a man like this.'

'Me? To be violent? I am an old man, Peter. And to be violent I must hate, and even this man Pike I do not hate.'

'It is not hate you need, Olav. It is love. You must gather your strength to protect yourself and your garden. The plants are your children, and even the most timid mother will act with all her strength to protect her children from a monster. She acts from love of her children not hate of her enemy.'

The old man listened to these thoughts carefully, hardly aware that he was being instructed.

'You are right, Peter,' he thought. 'I must be strong to protect myself and my children against this evil man. Come. I must clean my garden.'

'No, Olav. You must leave it. He has sprayed a poisonous mixture, lethal to your skin. The whole of the earth there is now spoiled and all the plants and creatures there are dead. There is nothing to do until the earth has drained the poison. Soon the soil will be clean again but until then you must wait.'

'I wait. As you say, Peter, I wait.'

And he did wait. And he never again questioned the boy. Nor did he ever again speak of him to anyone.

Meanwhile, although Mrs Wihongi had seen Michael Pike arrive and leave that morning, she had not seen the pump strapped to his back, nor the wand he carried low at his side and from which he sprayed the deadly poison to one side of the middle path on his walk up to the cottage, and to the other on his return to the car.

But she saw the awful result, guessed what had happened, and was terribly worried for the safety of her old friend.

Chapter 11.

"Pike was here yesterday morning. I saw him. He must have done it. He must have."

"In the morning you saw him?" asked Olav Kirsten.

"Too right I saw him, Olav," said Mrs Wihongi. "You can't miss that car you know."

She and Hone had come across to the old man before Hone went to school and the three of them were standing in the middle path with Brian. The garden lay as the old man had found it. Fearing the poison might still be active he had left it as the boy had said.

"He did it. I know," said the old man.

"You must call the police, Olav," said Mrs Wihongi.

"No, no, Mrs Wihongi. Is alright. He is crazy mad. He won't come again."

"But it's terrible what he's done," said Mrs Wihongi angrily. "It's dangerous isn't it, Hone? Hone knows about these things — these chemicals — Olav. You should let me call the police, shouldn't he, Hone. They'll know what to do if he is mad."

"No, no," insisted the old man. "Is alright now. Is alright."

"Mum's right, Olav," said Hone calmly. "We should call the police. With strong poison like that—" and he indicated to the black and rotting garden, "—anything could happen."

"No, no," insisted the old man. "Is alright now. Soon I will clean up this mess. Pike will not come back I think."

"But he might, Olav. That's the point. And then what would you do. He's mad that man. He should be locked up. Tell him, Hone. Tell him."

"If he comes I will fight him. I will give him something to pay him for his work," said the old man, chuckling.

"But, Olav," said Hone, unable to resist a smile. "What could you do — really — against such a bad person? You're an old man now."

"I will fight," said Olav Kirsten holding up a clenched fist. "The plants are my babies. I will fight like a mother for the life of my babies. Peter said—"

The other two noticed the unintentional mention of the boy's name.

"Well," said the old man, dropping his fist meekly, "I will fight this man if have to."

"What about Brian? Did he hear anything?"

The old man bent down to the old dog who lifted his head and closed his eyes while his old master rubbed his ears roughly.

"Is old now Brian. Tired and old and slow like Olav," said the old man. "But he growled, Hone. He growled and told me. But it was too late."

Hone walked back to the house with his mother and sat with her in the living room. He told her that the marae committee knew of Pike's reputation and was worried about the old man.

"But now they'll be angry, mum," he said. "They don't want the land sold. They said a big block of flats would bring in a lot of rates to the council, and prestige, and they think that could sway the council. A way to smarten up the neighbourhood sort of thing. But they don't like it."

His mother shook her head sadly at the thought of it all.

"A block of flats on Olav's garden," she said. "Oh, Hone, I can't believe it. What would your father think?"

"I rang up Greensborough you know," continued Hone. "Betty said I should."

"What did he say?"

"He's actually embarrassed about the whole thing but says there's nothing he can do. He says Pike's absolutely obsessed by Olav's land."

"Obsessed?"

"That's the word he used. Obsessed."

"Well I don't know what's going to happen, Hone," said Mrs Wihongi. "It's horrible that someone should be allowed to spray poison around like that. Horrible. Poor old Olav. He's never done anything to hurt anyone. Nothing. It's just not fair. And what about the people who depend on his vegetables. He gives it all away you know. All the stuff he grows. He just gives it away to people."

"I know, mum," said Hone. "I know. But he definitely doesn't want us to call the police, does he. You can tell that."

"No," said his mother. "But I will if anything else happens. I really will, Hone. It's not just Olav you know. Poison like that; well, anything could happen. What about that boy Peter who visits him?"

Hone nodded, thinking also of the primary school children who walk up and down Allison Terrace every day.

"Look, mum," he said "I'll tell you what. I'm going to get some of the guys from footie to help me. I'll get them to stay around here for a few nights, you know, to sort of guard the place. They all know Olav and like him. I'm sure they'll do it."

"Oh, yes, Hone," said Mrs Wihongi who thought the idea sounded very exciting. "Perhaps they'll even catch him red-handed."

"Yes. Well it might be worth it." Hone said. "We won't tell Olav. He won't have to know. We'll take it in shifts to sleep on the front porch. That'd be alright wouldn't it?"

"Oh, yes." Mrs Wihongi was very positive. "That's a wonderful idea, Hone. But they don't have to sleep on the porch. They can sleep in here on some stretchers."

"Well," said Hone, amused by his mother's enthusiasm. "It won't be tonight. I couldn't arrange it that quick. But tomorrow night, say.

64

I'll find out today but I think it'll be tomorrow night."

"Oh, yes, Hone," said Mrs Wihongi. "Tomorrow night. That'll be just fine."

But the next night was to be too late. For it was early next morning when Michael Pike paid his next visit to Allison Terrace.

The first pink streaks of the morning sun were sweeping up the eastern sky when his Rolls Royce stopped at Olav Kirsten's garden gate. Inside the cottage the old man lay on his back, his mouth open, breathing deeply. Beside him on the floor lay his dog, twitching slightly as he dreamed. The last sleep of the night lay heavily on the old dog and neither eye nor ear lifted even slightly as Pike slipped silently out of the car.

The morning autumn air was cold. He zipped up his sheepskin jacket as he stood on the road, holding the car door open slightly with his body. Then, secure from the cold, he reached into the car for the newspaper parcel that was lying on the passenger seat. Letting the car door rest on the lock, he tiptoed across the wet grass verge and stood looking over the stone wall at the property he was certain he would soon own. The destruction caused by his last visit was still evident — even in the dull light of dawn — and he was strangely glad to see the rotting and stinking vegetation lying on the surface of the poisoned earth.

Then, without wasting time, he carefully unwrapped the parcel he had brought from the car, and taking care not to touch it threw a lean and bloody steak half-way up the middle path. Then he got back into his car with the crumpled newspaper and left as silently as he had come.

The raw steak, juicy and tantalising bait for a hungry dog that only rarely tasted meat, lay for an hour where it had landed until the old man in the cottage awoke. Then he opened the cottage door, as he did every morning, so his dog could go outside to do what all creatures must do with more or less regularity.

Chapter 12.

It was cold in the hills of Rogaland but the evening sky was dark blue and cloudless, and there was no wind.

The streets of the ancient and tiny village, wet and dirty with melting snow, were deserted so there was no one to see the small dark boy, dressed in strange and foreign clothes, and without a jacket, scarf, hat or gloves, walking purposefully up the main street. Nor was there anyone to see him when he reached the crossroads, at the edge of the village, and turned left to begin the long climb up the stony path to the cemetery that was spread across the hillside. Looking back he could sometimes see, in the distance and between the blue hills, the steep and angry sides of the fjords, and the purple sea that lay, solid and unmoving, between them.

Before long he reached his destination. All around him was evidence of an ancient and pagan people who had buried their dead in these bleak and stony hills. But there were crosses, too, of a more recent time — for Christianity had come late to Norway — but most were in disrepair and many were fallen and broken. These lands once supported many more people.

He found what he was looking for, and stood in the evening chill studying the inscriptions on the headstones. Like their only son, Mr and Mrs Kirsten had each been blessed with a long life, and had died in the same year. There was no sign of their daughters, and the boy guessed that, if they were dead, and they probably were by now, they would be with their husbands, having their husbands' names which he did not know.

Then the boy was in the village seeking yet another place. There were a few more people out in the street now but they were mostly old. Indeed there seemed to be very few young people in this village. In the middle of the village, near the crossroads, was a grassy square with a statue in the middle surrounded by a stone wall. An old man was sitting on the wall resting his hands and chin on top of his walking stick.

"Are you a very old man?" asked the boy in the old language.

"Ja, my boy," replied the old man willingly. "I am ninety-eight years old."

"Do you remember the house of Olav Kirsten?"

"Ja. You want to go there?"

"I wish to see it. Would you show it to me please," said the boy quietly and politely.

Without getting up the old man pointed with his stick to the other end of the village.

"Take the lane after the village, on the left. It is one kilometre, only one house. It is just a small farm that old Olav Kirsten used to have."

"There were three daughters," said the boy.

"Ja. And a son. Young Olav. I remember him well. A little younger than I. A nice boy. But his angry father disowned him when he ran away to sea so he never returned."

"Did his father *never* forgive him?"

"Before he died he forgave him. The whole village knew about it. But it was too late. Too late. The boy was gone many, many years and nobody knew where he was."

"What about the daughters? Didn't they get married and have children? Where are all their children, and their children's children? Are they in the village?"

"The daughters of Olav and Margrete Kirsten and their husbands and all of their children are all gone. To America they went a long time ago," said the old man, remembering. "Everyone has gone from those days. Only I am left."

He was sad and lonely, the last of his generation, but he was pleasant, and he enjoyed talking to the strange boy who listened carefully before saying goodbye and making his way again through the village.

It was almost dark before he found what he was looking for: an old stone cottage sitting hard against the lane. The little farm was still there and still carried the mountain cattle of which he had heard his old friend speak many times. The cottage and the farm had changed little since that day, long ago, when a travelling photographer had posed the family so formally there on the ground in the middle of the narrow lane. The boy could see them there. He spoke to them — to the father and mother — of love and forgiveness, and then watched as they faded into the dark.

He stayed, looking at the cottage, until lights came on inside and threw long, sharp, yellow bands across the lane. And then, from the blackness of night, beyond the light, came a black dog with amber eyes. It was a young, handsome dog. His coat was glossy and his young muscles moved smoothly as he trotted briskly to the boy's side. But his head and tail were down. And he whimpered loudly as he stopped and lay at the boy's feet.

'Oh, Peter. Tragedy has struck our old friend again and now I am not there to comfort him. You must come at once. Come, Peter, please come.'

"He's gone again," whispered the nurse to the doctor who had just come into the room. "But he's been rambling a lot. Talking gibberish. Like a foreign language."

The old doctor nodded. Closing the door quietly behind him, he moved to the side of the bed. Stooping, he took a small, thin, limp, brown wrist in his hand and, watching his watch, counted off the pulse silently. Then, taking his stethoscope from the pocket of his baggy suit, he listened to the air and fluid that were jostling for space in the narrow chest.

Shaking his head sadly he pulled back the covers and injected a small measure of pain relief into the boy's thigh and, covering him again, turned to the nurse.

"Only a day or two, Molly," he said. "Perhaps less. You'll stay?"

"Of course," she said.

Glancing towards the closed door the doctor added: "They'll need you."

The nurse nodded. Understanding.

And then the doctor left. He had a large country practice, and a lot more calls to make that day.

Chapter 13.

After he had been let out of the cottage that fateful morning Brian began his day, as he always did, as is the habit and instinct of his species, with a careful inspection of the garden's boundaries. He was, after all, its guardian.

When he found the meat it was drier than it had been when Pike had thrown it there. It was dirty, of course, its edges had hardened, and much of the bloody juices had seeped into the moist dust of the middle path. Nevertheless, after smelling it carefully, the old dog picked it up and limped away to a quiet corner to cut it into edible pieces with his side teeth before swallowing it into his hungry stomach.

When he had finished he stood up, licked away the last taste from his loose black chops, and returned to the place where he had found the meat. There he sniffed at and around the spot thoroughly, to be sure that no meat remained, before walking slowly to the cottage door to rest.

But before he could cover even that short distance the morbid and powerful drug with which Pike had laced the meat was racing through the channels of his old body. When the pain came he was frightened and puzzled, curling his tail down between his legs. Then he fell heavily to his side, shaking and trembling terribly in the grip of a fierce convulsion. The poison acted quickly but, even so, the old dog's agony was great. Foam gurgled from his gasping, gaping mouth, his amber eyes stared horribly upwards, and he died when his breathing stopped and his heart burst in a desperate effort to pump freshened blood that didn't exist.

The muscle spasms continued even after he died so that his legs remained unnaturally straight and stiff, and his dead eyes remained open in a blind and horrible stare. Gradually, though, the muscles loosened and the old limbs lowered themselves slowly to the ground. But the foam remained around the mouth and on the ground, draining into the dust, and the fearful look remained in the open eyes. And there lay the old body until Olav Kirsten came out of the cottage to begin his day's work.

When he saw the dog, lying obviously dead in the middle path, he ran to him, crying with such anguish that Mrs Wihongi heard and came rushing from her house, her dressing gown flying hugely behind her.

She found the old man sitting in the dust of the middle path with the dog's head in his arms. He had used his sleeve to wipe the foam from the mouth and he had closed the dead eyes. He had put his head to the grey chest, seeking the thumping rhythm he knew he wouldn't find, and then, knowing that the dog was dead — and certain it was from a cause most unnatural — he rocked the animal lovingly in his arms, and wept.

He looked up when his kindly neighbour arrived. She saw the tears leaving his pale blue eyes, rimmed with red, and running down the creases and folds of his face, into his white beard.

"Is gone," he said, sniffing. "Brian is gone. To the Big Life he is gone."

Mrs Wihongi ached with pity for the sad old man looking up at her from the ground. But her anger was stronger.

"It's murder," she said bluntly. "He's murdered him."

The old man said nothing but returned his attention to the dead dog.

"Well I'm going to call the police this time, Olav," she said, retying her dressing gown, ready to bustle back to her own house.

"No! No!" called the old man. "Maybe later you call the police. Not now. Not now, please, Mrs Wihongi. There's nothing they can do now for Brian. It can wait the police."

Mrs Wihongi thought about it while the old man waited, looking up at her with wet and pleading eyes.

"Well, I'll make you a cuppa then," she said. "And I'll think about it." She sounded much more brave and determined than she felt. And she wished Hone were there.

The old man watched gratefully as she made her way up the middle path and into his cottage. He stayed with his dog, rocking him gently in his arms until, before long, Mrs Wihongi bustled out again with two mugs of hot tea. She dragged the old man's chair over to where he sat on the ground and, handing him one of the mugs, sat with him in the middle path in the early morning sun.

Together, and without words, they sipped the tea. The old man's tears had stopped, and he was lost in thought, but Mrs Wihongi was anxious and alert and she looked up quickly when she heard the sound of a big motorcycle growling its way up the street. She stood up when the noise stopped outside her own house and watched as it mounted the footpath and stopped at the old man's gate.

The rider got off his motorcycle and parked it on its stand. Seeing the two of them and the dog there, in the centre of the middle path, he opened the gate and marched towards them, his heavy boots clumping on the earthen path, until he stood at her side looking down at the old man and the dog.

Mrs Wihongi could see that his black leather suit was embellished with chains and metal decorations. And when he took off his dull black helmet she saw he had tattoos even on his face. His black, curly hair, once released from the helmet, stood out from his head, thick and long — she knew it was called an 'afro' — adding even more to his enormous height.

Mrs Wihongi was frightened. This was the biggest and fiercest bikie she had ever seen.

Chapter 14.

"What's going on, eh?" asked the big bikie as he looked from the old man and his dog to Mrs Wihongi, flicking his eyebrows up and down quizzically.

Olav Kirsten looked up silently but Mrs Wihongi stood up bravely, ready to protect her old friend against this mysterious new threat.

"What do you want?" she asked aggressively, but frightened by the face covered in dark and elaborate tattoos.

"Is alright, Doris," said the old man. "Is Little Timmy Tamatea. I know him. Long time. Hone knows him too."

"He does?" Mrs Wihongi was surprised.

The big Maori bikie squatted on his hams beside the old man, his leathers squeaking.

"Mr Kirsten," he said respectfully. "What's wrong here?"

Mrs Wihongi again noticed that he flicked his eyebrows up and down when he spoke.

"They killed his dog," she said bluntly.

"Yeah? That Pike joker?" asked Little Timmy, looking up at her.

"Yes. Probably," said Mrs Wihongi a bit more confidently. "How do you know about that, anyway?" she added.

"I was talking to Hone, eh. You know Hone? Oh, yeah. He's your boy, eh." And he quickly flicked his eyebrows up and down. "Well, I was talking to Hone and I was going to come and watch out for the old man tonight, you know. So I just come to see, eh. Check it out. Haven't been round here for a while."

Hone has some strange friends, thought Mrs Wihongi.

"What are yous fellas going to do now?" asked Little Timmy with the inevitable flicking of his eyebrows.

Mrs Wihongi shrugged and indicated with her eyes to the old man who was still sitting on the ground, with his dog, sipping quietly at his cup of tea. Timmy Tamatea was still squatting beside them.

"Leave him for a while, I suppose," she said. "Then I'm going to call the police."

"Don't call the pork," said Little Timmy. "Me and the boys can get that Pike joker."

"Oh, you can't do that. That's taking the law into your own hands."

"Why not? We do it all the time, eh," said Little Timmy. But he was smiling broadly. "Only joking, eh," he added with a flick of his eyebrows.

"Oh, you—" said Mrs Wihongi, laughing, and she gave the big bikie a friendly push on the shoulder enough to make him fall over. That made Timmy Tamatea laugh loudly — even the old man laughed at that — and Mrs Wihongi decided that she liked this Little Timmy friend of Olav.

Then another vehicle stopped on the street at the old man's gate. This time it was a huge rubbish truck. The driver and two runners left the truck idling noisily on the street and came up the middle path together. Although they were dressed differently from Timmy Tamatea — they wore brightly coloured shorts and football jerseys — they each equalled his height and, to Mrs Wihongi's eyes, his potential fierceness.

"G'day, yous fellas," said Little Timmy loudly, standing up and dusting down his leathers and picking up his helmet. Then he clumped down the middle path to greet the new arrivals. She sat on the chair and watched as the four men stood talking in a small huddle. She couldn't hear what they were saying but, afterwards, they all came and stood looking down at her, in her dressing gown, the old man and the dead dog.

"These are the other jokers that were coming round tonight," said Little Timmy, by way of introduction, and the three young men all nodded.

"We play footie with Hone," said one of them. "The Volcanoes."

"But you're so big. So much older than—"

"Hone's a big boy now, Mrs Wihongi," said the driver.

Then he knelt down and put his hand on the old man's shoulders.

"I'm very sorry this has happened, Mr Kirsten," he said with the same respect Mrs Wihongi had noticed in Little Timmy's voice.

Olav Kirsten looked up through reddened eyes, nodded and smiled, and the two other men also knelt down and gently patted the dead dog in wordless sympathy. Then, as quickly as they had arrived, they sprinted lightly down the middle path and were gone.

"You want a cuppa, Timmy?" asked Mrs Wihongi.

"Oh, yeah," said Timmy Tamatea. "Choice."

"No," said Mrs Wihongi. "Choysa."

And they both laughed and went into the cottage together to leave the old man on his own for a while.

'Olav. I am here now.'

'Oh, Peter. Is awful. Look at poor Brian. Is dead. From the poison I think. Like all the plants before.'

'It is good to cry, Olav,' thought the boy. *'But it is also good to remember that Brian has joined the Big Life again. Where he belongs. Where we all belong.'*

'You are right, of course, Peter. But Brian was my friend and I loved him in this life. That I can't help. Is natural. But I understand it he is in the Big Life now. Is good, I know.'

'It was Pike again,' thought the boy. *'He is a very sick man, Olav, to do this.'*

'He is an evil man, Peter,' thought Olav Kirsten. *'Evil.'*

'Olav. I will talk to you soon about things I have seen. Things I have learned. But it must wait. I cannot stay. I have been away a long time and now people are calling me. They are worried. I must go but I will see you again soon. Meanwhile you must return Brian to the earth where he belongs.'

'Yes. Soon, Peter, I will bury Brian. Not now but soon.'

The boy was gone by the time Doris Wihongi and Timmy Tamatea came out of the cottage. The old man had regained his composure and was standing now, wiping his eyes. His empty tea mug sat on the ground beside the dog; Mrs Wihongi picked it up.

"Little Timmy," said the old man to the bikie. "You are strong and big. You will help me bury Brian please."

"Sure, Mr Kirsten," said Little Timmy.

"You dig the big hole for me and I do the rest," said the old man. "In the weed garden. I will show you."

And he left Brian lying in the sun to fetch a spade and show his friend where to dig the grave. It was hot work for Timmy Tamatea, in his leathers, to dig such a deep hole. But he worked at it without stopping and, when it was ready, carried the now limp body to the edge and left it there for the old man.

"Is good," said Olav Kirsten to his friend. "Good, Little Timmy. Thank you. The rest I do."

Timmy Tamatea and Mrs Wihongi left him alone then. Sadly, but without hesitation or further tears, the old man lowered the dog's body into the hole, covered it with a sack, and using his hands at first, and then the spade, covered the body with the earth that Little Timmy had left in a mound beside the grave.

"I don't think he should have buried it," said Mrs Wihongi to Little Timmy as they were walking away. "It's evidence, isn't it."

"I dunno," shrugged Little Timmy as he headed out the gate towards his bike. "All I know is that you should tell Hone. Quick. He'll know what to do. I'll come back tonight, eh."

"Goodbye, Timmy," said Mrs Wihongi affectionately. "You're a good lad, you know." And she watched Timmy Tamatea put on his helmet, start his bike, and roar off down Allison Terrace towards Mount Eden Road.

Chapter 15.

The rest of the day passed slowly for Olav Kirsten. Once the dog was buried he began cleaning up the poisoned garden by raking the dead vegetation together, leaving it in a rotten and smelling heap.

Then he began the heavy, slow and tiring work of deeply digging over the soil of both rows, breaking it up and exposing as much of it as he could to the air, sun and rain. As he worked he thought constantly of Brian, his companion for so many years, who should have been lying somewhere nearby, watching him sleepily. And he thought of his other friend, the boy, and wondered who had been calling him, and what he had wanted to say. He was still working when Hone came home from school. Hone called out to his old neighbour but he received no reply.

"Olav's started cleaning up the garden," he said to his mother when he got inside.

And so his mother had to tell him what had happened to Brian; she told him about Timmy Tamatea and the men on the rubbish truck. They were sitting together in the kitchen.

"I didn't know you played footie with those jokers," she said. "They're so big, Hone. I keep thinking you're only a boy but—"

"I'll be at university soon, mum. And, anyway, it's not just footie. They're on the youth committee at the marae. I see them all the time."

"I don't know, son. I suppose you're the man of the house now."

Mrs Wihongi looked sadly at the photo of her husband that hung above the mantelpiece. Hone watched, knowing how much his mother missed him, his father. Then, suddenly, she remembered something.

"Oh, Hone. I nearly forgot. The police will be here soon."

"You rang the police?"

"Oh, son, I didn't know what to do. Olav didn't want me to call them but I thought I should. That man Pike, you know. He could be dangerous."

Hone stood up beside his worried mother and put his arm around her shoulder.

"I think you did the right thing, mum. No matter what Olav said."

They were still there when the two young policemen — Mrs Wihongi thought they looked especially young — knocked on the front door. She took them to the living room where Hone was waiting. She introduced Hone and they all sat down. One of them — Mrs Wihongi didn't catch their names at first — was very earnest, carefully writing notes in his little flip-top book while the other listened. She told them all she could about her neighbour, Olav Kirsten, and his garden. She told them about Betty Grey, and Michael Pike, and how she had seen Pike on the day of the plant poisoning and that although no one had actually seen him today, or last night, it must have been he who, somehow, poisoned to the dog.

"It must have been him," she insisted. "It's obvious. Hone thinks so too. He's so obsessed, that man."

"That may not be enough I'm afraid," said the young constable, the one who was not doing the writing. "You can't just go around making accusations like that without proof or evidence. Well, we can't anyway. The plants, now that's another thing. But you'd have to give evidence of that."

"In court you mean?" asked Mrs Wihongi.

"Yes. I'm afraid so," said the policeman. "And answer questions from a solicitor and all that."

"Oh, yes," said Mrs Wihongi with enthusiasm. "I'd be good at that wouldn't I, Hone. Anything to get that Pike."

"Yes," said the policeman. "Well, let's go and talk to the old man now."

Olav Kirsten was still digging over the poisoned soil when the four of them arrived but he stopped to answer the young policemen's questions, describing how he had found the dog, dead, with foam at the mouth.

"Sounds like poison alright," said the earnest constable.

"Is poison. Ja, is poison," said the old man. "That man Pike, he poison Brian."

"Yeah, well, it's not as simple as that, mate," said the policeman. "Where's the dog now? Can we see him?"

"No. Is buried now. In the weed garden."

"Buried? You buried him already?"

"Ja. Is dead. Little Timmy helped me bury him."

"Who's Little Timmy?"

"Little Timmy is my friend. He digs the hole."

"Well I'm sorry, Mr Kirsten, but we'll have to dig him up again."

Turning to Hone he explained that the dog's remains would have to be analysed and a full report given in evidence.

"If everything he says is true—"

"Is true. Is true," interrupted the old man. "He poisoned my garden first. Look. Now my dog."

"Yeah, well," continued the policeman. "If it's all true we're talking about a serious offence. There may be more than one charge here. That's a lot of legal palaver."

"You really need to dig up his dog?" Hone asked. It seemed such a cruel thing to do to the old man.

"Yeah. We'll need the dog definitely don't you reckon, Murray?" he said to his partner.

"We'll need the dog alright, mate," said Murray to Hone, the first words that Mrs Wihongi had heard from him.

"No," said the old man insistently. "No to dig up Brian now. Is too late. Too late."

"Well, it doesn't matter right now. We've got to put in our report and get statements from everyone first. But I think you'll have no choice when our report goes to town. It may be taken out of our hands, and yours I'm afraid, Mr Kirsten."

The old man nodded sadly.

"It sounds like it's getting really nasty now," said Betty when Hone and Mrs Wihongi told her about what happened.

"Oh, it is, dear," said Mrs Wihongi. "It's getting worse and worse."

"All the more reason to set the guard tonight," said Hone. "The others'll be around soon and we'll start about eight, when Olav puts out his light."

"Oh, yes, definitely. Definitely tonight."

"But what can I do?" asked Betty.

"You go home now, dear and we'll just leave everything to the men," said her mother. "Hone's in charge and I think he's doing a fine job."

She was very proud of Hone and the way he had organised his friends.

And so, early that evening, they all met in Mrs Wihongi's living room. Timmy Tamatea was still dressed as he had been that morning but the other three, the rubbish men, had come prepared for a cold night. Hone was amused to see his four friends sitting primly on the edges of their seats, each with a cup of tea on their knees, eating their way through a plate of his mother's Anzacs.

They discussed the events of the day and decided it was wise to set the guard for the next few nights. They agreed to follow Hone's plan to wait until the old man's light went off — Mrs Wihongi thought that would be about eight o'clock — and do five shifts of about two-and-half hours each finishing at half-past-eight the next morning.

"He'll be out in the garden by then," said Hone.

However, instead of sleeping on the porch, as Hone had suggested, Mrs Wihongi had them sleeping on stretchers in the living room. Eventually, when everything was ready, she went to the window and announced that the old man's light was out. And so the night's work began with Hone taking the first shift.

Chapter 16.

It was a cold, damp night but it passed without incident for the young men of the vigilante patrol. In accordance with the plan, the rubbish men left, to start work, when Little Timmy's shift started at six o'clock the next morning. Mrs Wihongi was up, had tidied up the living room, and had breakfast waiting for him when he finished at half-past eight. Hone was just leaving for school.

"Nothing happened, Timmy?" he asked the big bikie who was sitting down at the little kitchen table.

"Was pretty quiet all night," said Little Timmy, flicking his eyebrows.

"Okay. I'm off. I'll see you later. See you, mum."

"Bye, bye, dear."

"See you, bro," said Little Timmy.

"So what happened?" asked Mrs Wihongi when Hone was gone.

"The old man got up about six but he didn't see me. I was hiding, eh," said Little Timmy with a smile that lighted up his big, brown, tattooed face.

Meanwhile, in the cottage next door, Olav Kirsten was unaware of the precautions taken for him during the night. It had been an unhappy night, the first he had spent alone in the cottage, without Brian, for nearly twenty years. Now, as Little Timmy sat down to his breakfast in Mrs Wihongi's kitchen, he was outside continuing the unfinished task of turning over the poisoned soil. His heart was heavy, and he looked and felt a little older than usual. But he applied himself to his work willingly knowing that it would help relieve his sadness.

He worked steadily for nearly an hour, slowly and methodically pressing the large, heavy, steel spade into the lifeless earth, turning and breaking down each spadeful, leaving the soil as loose and light as possible. Even in his sadness he considered the therapeutic effect that the air, sun and rain would have on the soil, and how he, Olav Kirsten, would help bring it back to life with the help of his friends the worms from the compost.

He thought of the time — quite soon he hoped — when he would be able to take the tiny seedlings, already green and strong and waiting in their trays in the glasshouse, and press them with tender care, and individual affection, into the restored earth. He would talk to them, stroke and fondle them, watching their daily growth in the certain knowledge that nature, with her infinite patience, would return life to these two rows of dirt made so unclean by the greed of an evil man.

Olav Kirsten was sure that only a man with an unbalanced mind would have done what Michael Pike had done to him, his garden and his dog. He knew that Pike was beyond reason and that one day, for his own safety, he might have to raise his voice, or his fist, to this man.

Then he saw the familiar Rolls Royce stopping at his gate. He stopped his digging, and watched as Pike got out of the car and came towards the garden gate, a briefcase in his hand.

Olav Kirsten walked to the gate to meet the unwelcome caller.

"G'day, Mr Kirsten," called Pike with artificial friendliness. "Remember me?"

They met, one each side of the wicket gate. Michael Pike was smiling, holding his briefcase in his left hand as he held out his right.

The old man looked grim. He was holding his spade in his hand, blade upwards as if it were a spear. He did not accept the outstretched hand of the property developer.

"You dare to come again?" he said with quiet anger.

"Look, Mr Kirsten," said Pike, dropping his hand to his side. "Can't I come in and talk? There are things in here—" he tapped the briefcase, "—that I'm sure will impress you. There's nothing wrong with talking is there?"

"You killed my dog," said the old man sternly. His anger was increasing in the face of Pike's assumed cheerfulness.

"What do you mean I killed your dog?" Pike appeared astonished and hurt. "That's a terrible thing to say. You can't say that."

"And you poisoned my garden."

"Look, Mr Kirsten. I didn't come here to be accused and insulted like this. I'm a reasonable man and—"

"You are an *evil* man!" Olav Kirsten shouted.

The look on the old man's face was enough to frighten Pike who realised that he had gone too far. He began to back away from the confrontation, back towards his car.

"Come on," he said. "Surely we can talk about this like adults."

But the old man was truly angry now. He opened the gate and followed Pike as he backed towards his car.

"I love my dog and now is gone forever. Never to come back. Never." His eyes were wet again.

"Well you can get a new dog can't you?" said Pike, more anxious than ever to get to his car and away from this angry and threatening old man. "I'll buy you a puppy."

Olav Kirsten said nothing. His mood was very black.

He was moving forward more quickly now. As he reached the side of the car, the passenger side which was against the kerb, he lifted the heavy spade over his shoulder, like an axe, and swung it, with all his strength, into the passenger door panel of the Rolls Royce.

The fine old steel spade cut through the door panel with such ease that even the old man was surprised.

"Jesus Christ!" screamed Pike. "What the hell are you doing, you stupid old bastard!"

Furious and frightened, he dropped his briefcase and ran to the other side of the car.

Meanwhile the old man swung the spade again, this time into the car's rear door. Once again it tore through the sheet steel, tangling itself momentarily in the wiring and mechanism of the door. The old man levered it free, bending back the panel and tearing the steel even further.

"Oh, Christ!" screamed Pike again, and he leapt at the old man with vicious rage and hate. It was his insane intention to wrench the spade from the old man's hands and assault him with it until he was as dead as his dog.

Instead a thick, brown, tattooed arm was wrapped tightly around his neck as Timmy Tamatea lifted Michael Pike bodily off the ground and carried him, kicking and screaming, back to the stone wall where he dumped him heavily onto the damp grass and sat on him, laughing.

Chapter 17.

The nurse closed the bedroom door quietly and stood, her hands held loosely together in front, facing the old woman who was sitting in a corner chair with her eyes closed. She was the only remaining grandparent.

"It's over now," said the nurse. "I'm sorry."

The woman opened her eyes. She could hear her daughter and son-in-law sobbing together behind the closed door. She nodded, understanding.

"What do we have to do?" she asked.

"The doctor has to come. I'll go back to town. I'll tell the doctor. He'll come straight away to the wee boy. I promise."

"Thank you," said the old woman. There were tears in her eyes now. "And, Molly," she added. "Before you go could you ring Father McKay for us. I don't think I can do it right now."

The nurse smiled gently, and nodded. "Then I'll be off," she said. "Look after Marama and Toby now. They'll need help. It's going to hard for you all."

And when the nurse left the room to make the phone call the old woman stood up, raised her black eyes to the ceiling, and began an anguished and eerie wailing. It was the grief call of her people which she had learned before the nineteenth century was closed. Tuneless, and without rhythm, it was a terrible expression of deepest sadness. Ageless and eternal it said the dread of anyone who has been touched by death. It stirred the blood of the nurse, and she shivered involuntarily as she spoke to the priest. He heard it, too, as he had many times during his life in the North. Even over the phone it gripped his throat and he swallowed hard in order to speak.

The plaintive and ominous wailing of the old woman carried far, as it always had, as it was meant to, and reached the other children, five of them, some younger and some older than the dead boy, as they sat waiting in the long grass by the creek. Wordlessly they stood up, the eldest girl picking up the baby and resting it on her hip, and made their way sadly up the track, back to the house. In the village, Mac the mechanic heard it, too. He closed his garage and walked slowly up the unpaved road to his brother's house. And the kuia cried out in this way for a long time.

Chapter 18.

Mrs Wihongi and Little Timmy had run outside as soon as they had noticed the Rolls Royce arrive. Now, as Little Timmy continued to restrain Pike by sitting on him, and the old man stood beside the ripped doors of the Rolls Royce, the spade still in his hand, Mrs Wihongi stood at the edge of the little scene with her hands up to her mouth in horror.

Meanwhile a big orange rubbish truck had turned recklessly into Allison Terrace from the main road. The Rolls Royce had passed it earlier and now the driver pushed the heavy diesel truck to its limit while the runners hung on at the back, whooping and shouting with excitement. Slowing the huge vehicle as he reached the scene, the driver failed to stop in time and the rubbish truck smashed noisily into the back of the luxury car.

"Oops. Sorry but I meant it," he said.

Held down by the bulk of Timmy Tamatea, Michael Pike could only wince as he saw the back of his Rolls Royce buckle and rupture under the heavy steel of the truck's front bumper. Three little dolls, hooked gruesomely onto the truck's grill, nodded and bobbed with the impact, and then nodded and bobbed again as the driver backed up roughly to separate the two vehicles. Then the driver jumped out and joined his runners in front of Little Timmy and Pike.

"Hey, I'm sorry, Mr Pike," said the driver, mockingly. "I just didn't see your car there, eh. Must have had the sun in my eyes."

Little Timmy roared with laughter and rocked backwards and forwards on the whining and aching Michael Pike. Attracted by the noise, a small audience of neighbours had gathered at the scene. Housewives had come onto the street, and children had stopped on their way to school, and they were now standing about, staring, and talking excitedly amongst themselves. In the middle, sharing the crowd's attention with Timmy Tamatea and Michael Pike, stood Olav Kirsten, looking grave and ashamed, his spade still in his hand. Mrs Wihongi made her way to him and, walking with a weary stoop, he allowed her to lead him into the garden where, at last, he dropped his spade.

Once the old man was out of sight, and aware that the crowd was causing a problem, Little Timmy stood up and, hoisting up Pike by the belt of his trousers, he hooked him effortlessly over his hip and carried him back to the car where he stood him up beside the driver's door. Picking up the briefcase that was still lying where Pike had dropped it, Little Timmy took the speechless Pike's limp hand and closed his fingers around the handle.

"That's a real choice car, eh," he said to the stunned Pike who remained standing where he had been put. "Needs a bit of bog though, eh," he added with a flick of his eyebrows and a hearty laugh.

It was then that the police arrived, pulling to a fast stop behind the rubbish truck. It was the same two young constables who had called on Mrs Wihongi and the old man the day before. Having sized up the situation in advance they sprang from their car and set about their business without delay. One of them, the one that Mrs Wihongi knew was Murray, began by dispersing the neighbours and getting the children off to school while the other rounded up all those involved including the three rubbish men. Knowing they would never be able to sort things out on the spot the police called for another car and they all waited quietly on the footpath for it to arrive.

Olav Kirsten was taken in one car with Mrs Wihongi and Little Timmy.

"I've got to go with the old man," pleaded Mrs Wihongi, afraid she would be left behind.

"You have to come anyway, Mrs Wihongi. You're a witness to this shambles."

"Didn't do nothing, man," insisted Little Timmy. But they made him go anyway.

"You're a witness, too," they said.

The old man said nothing.

"Are you alright, Olav?" whispered Mrs Wihongi to her old friend.

"Is alright, Mrs Wihongi," said the old man, nodding. "But I have done a very bad thing. Very bad."

"Well never you mind about that now. It'll be all right, you see. I'm here and I'll look after you.

"But, Olav, wait till Hone hears about this."

Meanwhile, Pike and the three rubbish men were taken in the other car.

Once they arrived at the station the members of the group were removed to separate rooms. Despite Mrs Wihongi's protestations Olav Kirsten was left in a small room on his own. It was a drab and grey little room with only a small table and two hard chairs for furniture. The old man sat down alone, his hands between his knees. He felt tired and cool so he closed his eyes to rest, prepared for a long wait. He felt himself falling asleep. Then, just a few moments later, he was awakened by a small and familiar voice close to his ear.

'Olav.'

'Peter. Is that Peter? How are you to be here?'

'Olav. It's alright now.'

'Oh, Peter. Is awful what I do. I am ashamed.'

'Olav. You must understand. Everything is alright now. For all of us. Look who is here with me, Olav. Look.'

'Brian. Brian is here. How is Brian to be here?'

'Hullo, Olav,' said the young and handsome black Labrador.

'Brian. How is it you are talking? Oh, Brian.' And, weeping with emotion, he wrapped his

arms about the dog's neck. *'Peter. What is happening? These things I do not understand.'*

'Olav. Brian and I are here to take you away. Your mother waits. And your father, too. He has forgiven you, Olav. He has forgiven you and is longing to see you again.'

Chapter 19.

The death of Olav Kirsten in the Mount Eden police station made things complicated for the police, and when they found out that Michael Pike had disappeared — he was never seen again — it was clear that the whole episode was best forgotten.

But the news media wouldn't forget, and the next day one newspaper ran a front page story on 'The Life and Death of Olav Kirsten'. It condemned what it called his 'persecution' by a ruthless and greedy property developer, and called the police 'heartless' and 'uncaring' for leaving such a vulnerable and aged man alone in a cold cell.

Meanwhile Hone found he didn't have much time to be sad about the death of his old friend. Instead he spent the entire weekend working on his plan to save the old man's garden from development knowing that soon after the funeral the council was going to demolish the cottage and clear the land in readiness for the auction. He knew he had to stop that from happening. He knew that the mana of his father's people, of his marae, and of a good and wise man, were now a part of that land.

He knew that Olav Kirsten had loved his land and had understood, like the Maori, that it wasn't there to be divided and sold for profit. He knew that, after a time, the land of the people becomes part of the people, owned by none but belonging to all. He knew that it becomes a part of life — the Big Life as Olav called it — and, for generation after generation, should be tilled and turned and trod upon with reverence and respect.

But what could he do?

He spent a lot of time discussing the problem with the Maungawhau marae committee but even together — he and all the adults — they couldn't see a solution. The land must be sold in accordance with the old man's will. That was the law.

Hone outlined his plan to raise the money to buy the land now, before the auction, but the committee couldn't see how it could be done in time. He went with Betty Grey to the town clerk's house and the town clerk confirmed what he already knew: that as soon as possible after the funeral the council was going to move men in to demolish the cottage and tidy the land before holding the auction.

"As the council sees it," said the town clerk, "it has a duty to follow the old man's will: look after the land, get the maximum possible price, recover the overdue rates, and pass on the profit to—"

"To the marae," interrupted Hone. "Can't you see? The marae doesn't want the money. The marae just wants to preserve the land."

"Yes, young man, but listen," said the town clerk. "You're not supposed to know about the money and the marae." And turning to Betty Grey he said: "I should never have told you that, Betty."

"Well you did and it's too late now," said Hone. "But can't you see? It doesn't make sense."

"It makes sense to the council, Hone. We have to get the rates arrears. That was the arrangement."

"But what if I could pay the rates. I'll find a way. I'll raise the money."

"Come on, Hone," said the town clerk. "You're dreaming. Even if you could it'd cause a terrible scandal if the council didn't go through with the agreement."

Hone also found that the Olav Kirsten had an exaggerated view of the borough council's importance, and had appointed the town clerk to arrange his funeral. In his own well-meaning way the town clerk had arranged a small chapel service followed by a cremation. At least Hone was able to convince him that he had under-estimated the probable attendance at the funeral, and eventually the town clerk agreed to move the service to a large church in the shopping centre. But he couldn't get him to change his mind about the cremation.

"He should be buried," Hone insisted.

"Why?" asked the town clerk.

"Because he should be, that's all. He wouldn't like a cremation."

"He left the arrangements to the council, Hone. And council is encouraging cremations. It's much more practical. And healthy."

"Healthy?"

"What's wrong with cremation anyway?" asked the town clerk.

"Look. I know — knew — the old man really well," said Hone. "All my life. Can't you understand that? He believed in, well, 'things', that's all. Tikanga. Maori things. I just know he would rather be buried. In the earth. It's the way of our people."

"But he isn't one of your people, Hone."

Finally, on the Monday morning, Hone Wihongi had a new idea. He didn't go to school that day but spent most of it at home, on the phone. This time he forgot the 'important' people from whom, thus far, he had been seeking help. Instead he spoke to those ordinary people who, he believed, had reason to be grateful to Olav Kirsten.

He wasn't asking for much: only that they come to the old man's funeral on the following day.

"Let's give him a real tangihanga," he said, and even the most urbanised of them understood that.

"We'll be there, Hone," they all said. "For the old man's sake, we'll be there."

There were a few people whom he had to see in person and he called on them at their homes, their jobs, wherever they might be. Such was the affection that the people of Mount Eden had for old Olav Kirsten and his garden that, without exception, young Hone Wihongi and his plan were both warmly received.

At last, at the end of the day, Hone knew that the old man's land would be safe from development whatever the council said or did. There remained only one more thing to do, and he waited until it was dark before going next door to meet Timmy Tamatea and the three rubbish men in the middle path of Olav Kirsten's garden.

Chapter 20.

It was a large funeral, the largest seen in the district for many years. The little coffin lay on a simple wooden table in the centre of the great whare whakairo which itself lay, with outstretched arms, on the green and flat land that was the marae beside the river. On a hill behind the meeting house stood the tiny church, ornately decorated in the local style. From the low front door of the church the graveyard — older than this church — spilled down the hill towards the river and the road, and then, in the other direction, climbed randomly up the hill towards the bush.

High on the hill, close to the bush, was a new hole, black and shiny and wet, and beside it stood a hillock of mud, heavy with the rain. As they arrived the groups of mourners averted their eyes from the cemetery, concentrating instead on the familiar meeting house and the warm, human and very live activity taking place within.

As each visiting party left its car it was greeted by the traditional and melancholic call that stretched out thinly and painfully through the rain, across the marae and the car-park, to reassure them that they were at the right place and that they were welcome.

Old men and women, steeped in the customs of their race, raised and lowered their arms, and gave soft voice, in an instinctive response to the welcome. Some women had greenery braided into their dresses and shawls; they carried small branches that they raised in the air and brushed against their legs to depict the way their ancestors would beat themselves, drawing blood, to show their distress at the loss of such a loved one.

Many times that morning did the awful but welcoming chant cut through the light rain and across the grass. And still, apart and above, could be heard the eerie lament that the women voiced when their pouri, their awful grief, was too much.

Many, too, were the Pakeha who were greeted. Some, like Father McKay and the doctor, were offered the hongi, pressing noses and thus sharing vital air with the people who stood to the side of the coffin.

When everyone was assembled, Toby and his brother lifted the coffin lightly and carried it, behind the priest, out of the meeting house towards the road. Behind them came the kuia, the grandmother, and then behind her walked the mother carrying the baby, and the other children behind her, while the rest of the whanau fell in behind and formed a long procession out onto the road, along to the church path, and eventually up to the church itself.

During the procession, through the drizzling rain, the kuia again voiced her bitter and primeval song. Spontaneously, when compelled by their emotions, other women, too, would add their laments to cross and join and then leave the old woman's voice, making arcane harmonies that only they could hear. Then, suddenly, they would all stop and the grandmother would continue alone.

At last they arrived at the church. Because there were so many people many had to stand outside in the rain. It was eleven o'clock and they joined Father McKay in requiem mass.

Finally, the short journey from the church to the grave was led by the old priest. As the people gathered around he intoned the words that his church said were appropriate to the moment. But again the people found better expression in the wailing of the ancient chants that floated to the end of misty valleys to haunt the bush, and the dreams of men, forever. And so stood that group of old and young, family and friends, as father and uncle knelt in the cool autumn rain to lift the wet mud by hand and begin their dreadful duty.

Only the kuia noticed the old Pakeha with the white beard, a black dog at his side, standing in the rain at the edge of the bush. He seemed to nod to her when she caught his eye but her own eyes were old, cloudy, and wet with tears, and when she blinked, and looked again, he was gone.

But she remembered.

Then it was over, and they walked home together through the rain. The old woman's wailing had stopped and she held on to the arm of her wet and muddy son-in-law, walking slowly with her stick because she was tired and cold. The family walked slowly, too, so as not to tax her.

"Hey, Hunaonga, it is good to be finished," she said, in her first language, looking up at her son-in-law. "My mokopuna Pita, he was very sick."

The son-in-law and father nodded sadly.

"But now he is returned to the land of his people," she said. "For that he is lucky. Before today his wairua left him many times. Now it is gone forever and his body rests."

She pointed to the wet mud and clay that covered the man's hands and was smeared on his clothes. She pointed but did not touch.

"I am glad you have mixed with the earth of his grave. It is good for us all. But you must not wash for many days. And your kakahu, you must not clean them. Not yet. Marama will know when."

"Yes, hungarei," said the young man respectfully.

"And kai. You must let Marama feed you. You must."

"I will do what you say, old woman," he said, respectfully, in Maori. "But why? I try but I don't understand the old ways."

The old woman stopped in the middle of the road, and all the whanau stopped and gathered around to hear her words. Standing in the rain, she spoke in English for the sake of the young people who were being pressed to the front by their elders.

"My mokopuna Pita was very young," she said quietly. "But, believe me, my son-in-law, his wairua was very old, very wise, and much travelled.

"Even today, at the edge of bush, in the rain—" and she paused, closed her eyes, and remembered the look on the old Pakeha's face.

She opened her eyes and now spoke more forcefully and with great authority.

"He had great mana," she said, looking around at her family, "from his whanau, from his matua, his father and mother, but also from himself."

"But still I don't understand, hungarei," said the grieving father.

The old woman used her stick to point at the mud thick on her son-in-law's hands and suit.

"The oneone of his grave," she said. "It must be sacred to his family forever."

Then she looked directly up into his face.

"Tapu, Hunaonga," she said gravely. "Tapu."

And the man heard, and shivered, and nodded solemnly, remembering the teachings of his own tupuna many years ago.

Chapter 21.

St. Martin's was the borough's largest church; it still stands, in its own grounds, in the middle of the shopping centre. A wide bitumen path, flanked by an avenue of bulky Phoenix palms, leads from the front door to the busy main street, and it was at that door, on that rainy day, that the black hearse stood waiting to carry the body of Olav Kirsten to the crematorium.

Inside the church the atmosphere was cold and sombre. An old woman in a purple coat, sitting at a cheap organ, was releasing that instrument's most plaintive notes and chords, and the noise echoed loosely around the varnished wooden walls.

The coffin, Olav Kirsten's coffin, stood at the front of the church. Its dark and polished wood was embellished with ornate metallic handles, and a wreath sat stiffly on the lid.

Hone was nervous. He was sitting near the front of the church with his mother. The funeral was about to begin — at eleven o'clock — and the church was full. He looked around. At the back he could see the men from the funeral parlour waiting to lift the coffin and carry it to the hearse. He could also see Timmy Tamatea sitting conspicuously in the back row. He nodded to the bikie who flicked his eyebrows up and down in silent acknowledgement. Beside

110

Little Timmy were the three rubbish men, dressed conservatively in dark suits. They, too, soberly acknowledged his nod.

He saw his other friends: the kuia, who pretended not to see him, and, at the very back, the entire Edenside senior rugby-league team — the Volcanoes — sitting quietly with their hands in their laps. He wondered if they were all as nervous as he. But it was too late for second thoughts; they were all committed.

It had seemed like such a good idea yesterday, Monday, when he had spoken to them all. But now he was less confident. And he didn't have the support of the marae committee.

The organ stopped and Hone's heart raced. He clenched his fists. Not long now. Not long.

The minister emerged from a side door and walked briskly to the centre of the altar where he stood in front of the coffin. He began the service at once, routinely reciting the standard service, much of it from memory. His delivery showed that he had not known Olav Kirsten and did not know of the deep respect felt for him by the Maori people of Tamaki-makaurau. A hymn was sung after which the congregation sat down noisily for a reading from scripture.

Then the organist pressed out an opening chord and the congregation rose for the second hymn, the Twenty-third Psalm.

"The Lord's my shepherd,
I'll not want,
He maketh me down to lie,

In pastures green,
He leadeth me—"

Hone's time had come. He turned and nodded towards the back of the church. At once the kuia lifted her quivering hands high and, in discordant contrast to the old English hymn, began her own more ancient lament. It was a dissonant, harsh and shocking sound: the piercing and chilling notes slipping up and down their own scale, ignoring all European musical convention.

The congregation stopped singing and turned to stare at the old Maori woman who continued her wailing unselfconsciously. The organist stopped playing and looked at the minister for guidance but the minister didn't know what to do either.

Hone waited. He clenched his fists again. Waited. And hoped. The dreadful Maori lament was the only sound in the otherwise hushed church. Then the mystical and ancient music did what it has always done and loosened the voice of another woman. Hone didn't know who she was but she joined the lament, matching and answering the power of the kuia's cry.

Then another began.

Hone unclenched his fists at last. It's working, he thought. It's working. And his mother — weeping but smiling — nudged him with her elbow.

The minister held up his hands for quiet but the request was ignored. Two of the funeral director's men stepped from the porch into the body of the church but were blocked by two Volcanoes who, with hands flattened against the men's chests, pressed them gently and easily back into the porch.

Soon the church echoed with the wailing of many women and the power of their mourning overwhelmed the sedate Anglican service. Many people were crying and lifting their arms in the traditional manner, grateful for the intensity of the tangihanga and the relief it brought.

When Hone turned and nodded again Timmy Tamatea and the three rubbish men acted quickly and together. To the amazement of the people in the pews around them the four young men stripped off their jackets and shirts, completely baring the tops of their bodies, and marched together down the aisle towards the coffin. Once again the funeral director's men stepped into the church and once again the big Maori Volcanoes stopped them. But this time they took them outside and threw them unceremoniously onto the wet grass.

That stirred the television camera crews and newspaper photographers, already made curious by the unchurchly sounds, who were waiting impatiently in the churchyard, trying to avoid the rain. Then the television cameras started, and the press cameras flashed, when four huge, muscular, half-naked men, carrying the coffin of Olav Kirsten lightly on their broad, brown shoulders, came slowly out of the church and down the stairs. Behind them came the wailing women followed by more people, Maori and Pakeha, answering the call of the kuia.

Now, ahead, on the grass, twenty bare-chested Volcanoes were standing straight and tall in the cold. As the coffin moved past them — and as the television cameras rolled — they spread their legs and bent their knees and gave of their fiercest to the only haka they all knew. Their deep, manly voices called out in unison, with exaggerated anger, the bragging words of the defiant warrior, Te Rauparaha:

> *Ka mate, ka mate,*
> *Ka ora, ka ora,*
> *Ka mate, ka mate,*
> *Ka ora, ka ora,*
> *Tenei te tangata*
> *puhuru huru,*
> *Nana nei i tiki mai,*
> *Whakawhiti te ra,*
> *A upane, ka upane,*
> *A upane, ka upane,*
> *Whiti te ra.*
> *Hi!*

And as they called out they stamped their feet to show how they would crush their enemies' skulls into the earth like moa eggs; they slapped their hard thighs to emphasise the muscles and sinews that could carry them swiftly on attack. Bending one arm, then the next — their fists in the air — they looked proudly down at their muscles, slapping them loudly to draw attention to their great strength. Pushing forward their chests they slapped them rhythmically, noisily and hard to raise their heart and their lungs and their anger to the highest pitch. And throughout it all they distorted their faces to ugliness, with much rolling of the eyes and quick darting of the tongue, to prove that these were, indeed, enraged and savage warriors who would not be stopped from doing what they must do.

And then, with a final violent leap, they threw their hands to the sky and, with rhythmic grunts, joined the funeral procession, the head of which was out of the church grounds and turning into the main road.

Chapter 22.

Leaving his mother, Hone hurried to the front of the procession to join Little Timmy and the rubbish men. Together they led the long funeral procession off the footpath and into the centre of the wide and busy main road. Traffic stopped, as it had to, to let the procession pass. People stared. Some, knowing that this must be the funeral of Olav Kirsten, left the footpath and joined the lengthening line.

Then other people joined in, people who had nothing to do with the old man. A Ngapuhi bus driver was moved to tears by the sounds he had not heard since he was a child; hearing the call of his people he left his bus — and his passengers — and ran to join the line, stripping off his shirt and tie as he ran.

Others saw and followed his example. The driver of a concrete truck left his machine. A man who owned a dairy ran out of the shop, calling his wife to take care of it while he was gone. A taxi driver locked his cab and left it on the rank. They all took off their shirts in imitation of Little Timmy, the rubbish men and the footballers. Because, to them all, it seemed tika, the right and Maori thing to do.

Led by Timmy Tamatea and the rubbish men, their hard, brown bodies glistening in the rain, the long procession moved, with stately and swaying slowness, up Mount Eden Road, into Allison Terrace, and up the gentle slope of Olav Kirsten's beloved mountain towards his garden. Still the women cried and called out, and still the rain fell as it fell all over the country that day. The television crews had radioed for help and now there were three vans cruising the length of the line. Press photographers were there, too, ignoring the rain to get the dramatic picture each hoped would be on his paper's front page.

Hone, his shirt discarded, walking beside Little Timmy at the head of the line, smiled inwardly, thinking of the pressure the news film and press photos would put on the borough council. Wally Greensborough was there, in the middle of the line. Like many of the men of Maori descent he had stripped off his shirt to walk bare-chested through the rain. He was smiling to himself, too, thinking of the audacity of the young Hone Wihongi, the high school student whom he had not yet met.

Good on you, boy, he thought. Bloody good on you.

The town clerk was there, and Betty Grey, and the people from the museum and the university. So were the two policemen who were uncertain whether what was happening was legal and, if it were not, what they should do about it. Unsure, they decided to stay with the procession to see what happened.

The area around the hole which Hone, Little Timmy and the three rubbish men had dug the night before, in the middle path of the garden, was soft and muddy by the time the coffin bearers had come through the gate. Without hesitation they carried their burden up the middle path to the grave where they lowered it to the muddy earth and stood back. The Volcanoes formed a circle around them and they all waited as the procession continued to file into the garden.

At last the minister arrived. Now, at last, he seemed to understand the importance of the morning's events and, brushing aside the funeral director, hurried through the gathering crowd to the graveside. Someone held up an umbrella for him, and he opened his prayer-book to begin the burial service with renewed sincerity.

Then, as Little Timmy and his three friends used ropes to lower the coffin into the muddy grave, someone in the crowd — a crowd that now filled every available space in the garden — began the hymn that had been rudely interrupted at the church. As hundreds of voices were lifted to the black sky that hung so depressingly on the mountain, Hone Wihongi was the first to lift a handful of damp and sticky Mount Eden volcanic dirt and drop it into the hole. Others followed, and soon there was a line of people wanting to get the dirt of Olav Kirsten's garden onto their hands.

But only the frail kuia — exhausted from the long march, and standing at the graveside with

Mrs Wihongi and Hone, gripping Hone's arm for support — only she saw the small brown face at the cottage window. She wondered if it was one of Hone's school children and, if so, why he wasn't at school. Why was he in the cottage? She went to tug Hone's sleeve to show him but the boy in the window smiled, just a little, and shook his head as if to say 'no'. She smiled back, understanding and tranquil, knowing with complete confidence that an atua was there watching over them. She looked up at Hone and patted his arm affectionately. And when she looked back to the window the boy was gone.

Meanwhile Mrs Wihongi was also watching the cottage. Unable to stop the television cameramen from climbing onto its roof to get a better view of the scene, she decided to make a personal check of the inside knowing that only she had a key. Unnoticed by anyone she unlocked the door and slipped inside.

Standing inside, alone, she could hear the mixed sounds of rain and scraping feet on the tin roof above and, from the garden, the strains of the beautiful old hymn. She looked around sadly: everything was just as Olav had left it. She found it hard to believe that it was only Friday that Pike had arrived and that she and Little Timmy had gone rushing out to stop him, in his rage, from killing the old man. And then Olav had died anyway. Like Brian. Gone forever.

She thought about Hone and his plan. She was proud of her son but she wasn't sure that his plan would succeed. She still felt that the council would demolish the cottage, Olav's cottage, and auction the land. And then what would be left? Nothing. Because there was nothing in the cottage of importance or value to anyone but the old man.

She was about to leave when she heard a noise behind her; something falling on the floor. She turned and saw something — two things — on the rug beside Olav's bed. How, she wondered, did they get there? How did they fall? She went to them, picked them up and — deciding quickly — slipped them both into her handbag. Then she left the cottage quickly, for the last time, locking the door behind her.

Outside, Hone, Little Timmy and the rubbish men had almost filled in the grave. Most of the large crowd had left the garden and were drifting down Allison Terrace. She found Betty and together they collected the people they thought should come to her house for a cup of tea. Even Wally Greensborough and the town clerk were invited and, before long, they were both locked in debate with the whole marae committee in her living room. The rubbish men came in at last for their cup of tea, and that left only Hone and Little Timmy in the garden, all according to plan. But they were not entirely alone. The television crews, sensing a big story, had stayed. And so they filmed everything that happened there, in that garden, on that historic day.

Working without speaking, Hone and Little Timmy carried two long and stout poles from behind the cottage and set them into the holes each side of the gate. Then they brought the props and stakes they had prepared the night before and, taking time to do a good and permanent job, used them to fix the poles upright and rigid.

Only when they were sure that the poles, now straight and high in the air, were set firmly enough into the ground, did Hone fetch the last few items of equipment. Then, with Little Timmy's help, he stood on the wall and, using battens, nailed one of his mother's sheets to the poles to form a banner stretched tight and high above the opening of the gate.

Finally, as the television crews knelt below him on the wet street, filming upwards, Hone Wihongi took a can of black spray paint from Little Timmy and, in letters as tall and bold as he could fit on the sheet, painted one word:

T A P U

Chapter 23.

For two days and nights Timmy Tamatea stood watch alone, under the sign at the garden gate, to stop anyone who might arrive to start work on the demolition of the cottage and the preparation of the land for sale.

But no one came.

It wasn't because the council had changed its mind; it hadn't. But after the story of Olav Kirsten and his garden had been broadcast on network television, after its significance had been investigated and analysed by experts, after the young Hone Wihongi had been interviewed standing in front of the sign, after the newspapers had editorialised about the stuffiness and inflexibility of the council, there was no one in the country who would dare set foot on the tapu land of Olav Kirsten.

No bulldozer driver could be found who was prepared to enter the property and work the land. And even if one could be found, there was no truck driver willing to deliver his machine. Men in building and construction firms made it clear to their employers that they would have nothing to do with the tapu garden in Mount Eden. Even the unions got involved and it amused Hone to hear union officials speaking of tangi and tapu and Maoritanga in the ugly and clumsy accents of England and Scotland.

Finally, when even the council's own staff refused to work at the site, a special council meeting had to be called.

At the meeting the town clerk described to the councillors what he had learned from his discussions with Wally Greensborough and the marae committee at Mrs Wihongi's: there was a way to satisfy everyone. He explained that Mr Greensborough, of Greensborough and Pike, a very rich man, was prepared to buy the land, repay all the overdue rates, and give — yes, give, the town clerk had to emphasise — the land to the Maungawhau marae. In return, he continued, the marae had promised to turn the land into a public park for the benefit of the entire neighbourhood providing only that they could fence off the grave of Olav Kirsten.

In this way, explained the embarrassed town clerk, the councillors could be seen to be doing their legal duty to the old man by selling his land for as much as they could get — Wally Greensborough was prepared to pay a very handsome price — and, after deducting the overdue rates, could pass the surplus onto the marae. The council would get its overdue rates, the marae would get the remainder of the money as the old man wanted, the land would be preserved intact in accordance with the will of the people, and no single property developer would be seen to be given an advantage. Thus there was no room for scandal.

The opinion of the councillors at the meeting was that, until then, they had been badly advised by their town clerk; they found that he had been outmanoeuvred and outwitted by a high school student, that his clumsy management had put them in an embarrassing position, and that the resulting publicity was unwelcome in their little borough.

They wanted the problem solved.

Thus they embraced his solution and dismissed him from the meeting. He was instructed to stay out of the affair until the mayor and the chairman of the parks committee had sorted it out with the marae committee; his only remaining duty was to telephone Mr Wally Greensborough to tell him that his proposal had been accepted.

"Hone. I've got to talk to you after the meeting."

Hone Wihongi nodded. He was at a youth club meeting at the marae. Afterwards he sat down in the coffee shop with his school friend, Bonnie Hotere.

"Hone. It's really weird. Strange." Her black eyes stared deeply into his.

"What is?"

"Look, I couldn't go to Olav's funeral. I would have but I just couldn't."

Hone shrugged. "Doesn't matter."

"Hone. I had to go to another funeral. A real old tangi up north. Like the old days. It was really strange. Like the old people always say. My God, it even rained."

She took a sip of coffee, nervously, and continued:

"You remember my cousin Marama? It was her little boy. You remember? He stayed with us last year when he was having treatment up at Auckland Hospital?"

"He went to school one day," said Hone, remembering.

"Yeah. That's the point," exclaimed the excited woman.

But Hone was puzzled. "What's the point?" he asked. And then: "What was his name again?"

"Pita," said Bonnie with a distinct Maori pronunciation.

"Pita. Of course. Not Peter." Hone smiled broadly. "Pita. Pita."

"What's the joke?"

"Nothing," said Hone. "What else?" He was interested now.

"Well," the young woman continued quickly, "last year Pita was sick and he stayed with us to have the treatment. Olav used to bring stuff around and that. Vegetables. You know what he was like. But he and Pita never actually met.

"Then one day, when Pita was feeling okay, he went to school with Simon — my little brother — and their class went to Olav's with you and Betty. Don't you remember?"

Hone shook his head.

"Well he did. And, Hone, he never forgot. *Never.* He used to talk about the old man all the time. And the dog, what was his name?"

125

"Brian."

"Yeah. Brian, too. He talked about them all the time. Even in his sleep. Even when they thought he was unconscious. And then, finally, he died. Poor little joker. Last week. A week today, Friday. And I went to the tangi all weekend—" she was speaking quickly now "—and the funeral was on Tuesday and Marama told me all about it. How Pita used to talk about Olav in Mount Eden all the time. And the dog. And Marama wanted to be sure that when I got back to Auckland I'd go and tell the old man — that's what she called him — that Pita had died. You know, because he seemed so important to Pita."

She finished her coffee before continuing, more slowly now.

"But then we saw it on TV. The old man died, too. And we saw what happened, what you did and all that. I mean that was really terrific, Hone. The Maoris up north—" she looked heavenward, "—they think you're a real hero, eh."

"Yeah. Well, what about Pita though?" asked Hone.

"Well, don't you *see*? Don't you get it? I figured it all out on the way home. So did Marama and Toby."

"What?" Hone was getting impatient.

"Well, little Pita and old Olav. First of all they must have died about the same time on that same day, Friday. Don't you see? But then, not only that, their funerals were at exactly the same time on the same day: eleven o'clock last Tuesday."

Hone nodded.

"Well don't you think that's a pretty weird coincidence, Hone? Pretty strange? The kind of *weird* thing that used to happen, you know, in the old days. I tell you what: I wouldn't want some of the old people around here to hear about it. They'd say it was an omen or something, don't you think?"

"Yeah. They probably would," said Hone. "And they might be right, Bonnie, you know."

"Oh, come on, Hone. Big, important Maori like you. Big shot on TV, eh." And she punched him affectionately on the shoulder.

"He never came back to Auckland did he?"

"Who?" Bonnie finished her coffee.

"Pita. The boy."

"No. Of course not. He was too sick after that. Went to Whangarei hospital once. That's all. Needed constant nursing. Marama was under an awful strain. He couldn't go anywhere."

"But he couldn't have come back to Auckland for more treatment or anything? Like without you knowing about it?"

"No. I told you. He was too sick. Come on, Hone. He was dying. Why, anyway?"

"Well, it's even stranger than you think, Bonnie. Much stranger," said Hone.

"Is it?" said Bonnie, intrigued. She leaned forward. "Tell me more."

So Hone told her about the mysterious little friend Olav called Peter. And when he had finished he told her how Olav had thought that the boy came from Edenside school. How he had visited Olav frequently over the last few weeks although none but Olav had ever seen him.

"But I checked, you know, pretty carefully," he said. "There are no Maori kids called Peter, or Pita for that matter, not at Edenside. This year or last year. But I forgot all about your Pita. I didn't even think about him.

"I mean, just one day? Just one visit to Olav?"

Bonnie Hotere leaned back on her chair.

"Wow." she said. "That's a freaky story, Hone. Really amazing, eh. Someone should write it down. You know, in a real book."

Epilogue

Under instructions from his mother Hone hammered two small nails into the kitchen wall above the mantelpiece, one each side of his father's portrait. Then, as he waited on the stepladder, his mother handed him up two small framed pictures and supervised from below as he hung them on the nails and set them straight.

He came down to view the pictures properly, and his mother stood with him, taking his arm.

"He would have liked that, Hone," she said. "They look nice, don't they. Some company for your father."

Hone gave his mother a hug.

"He would have been proud of you, you know, Hone," she said. "I know I am."

But that was long ago. Mrs Wihongi is very old now — almost as old as Olav Kirsten was when he died — but quite well. She still lives alone in the same house in Allison Terrace, and the faded pictures still hang on her kitchen wall, where Hone put them, to remind her of her old neighbour.

Every day she walks through the park that was once Olav's garden, stopping at the black iron fence of his grave. His cottage is gone — it was taken down when the tapu was lifted — and she senses that all is not yet perfectly well in this quiet little corner of Mount Eden. It's as if the little park is asking for patience; as if it needs to be left in peace for just a few more years. And although all who visit there can sense it, few know why it should be so.

Hone thinks he understands. And so does his friend, Bonnie Hotere. And the aged kuia, who once saw a little brown face in a dark window, went to her own grave knowing that the garden of Olav Kirsten, once the garden of her own people, would be tapu whenua forever.

The end

Glossary

The Maori language, like all living languages, contains many words which have more than one meaning and where the often subtle differences are so fine they can be properly discerned only in context. This simple glossary is meant to assist the reader in understanding the Maori words which occur in this book only in the sense that they are used in this book. Note that macrons are conventionally used in printing the Maori language but, given the limited purpose of this glossary, their use here was not seen as necessary.

Atua	God, spirit or deity.
Haka	Traditional dance, often performed by men, now performed ritually on special occasions especially by New Zealand sports teams.
Hongi	Maori form of greeting involving the pressing of noses and the symbolic exchange of vital air.
Hunaonga	Son-in-law.
Hungarei	Mother-in-law.
Kai	Food.
Kakahu	Clothes.
Kauri	A conifer tree, *(Agathis australis)*, native to New Zealand but related to trees of the same genus throughout the Western Pacific. The mature New Zealand kauri is one of the largest trees in the world.
Kuia	An old woman, usually much respected for her mana.
Mana	A word, without an English equivalent, implying the power and influence derived not from a person's office or title but from the esteem in which they are held by others without coercion.
Marae	Originally an open space associated with the Maori village and pa acting as the focal point of the community's social life. It still means an open space set aside for Maori assembly, including the buildings

131

and facilities, although the members of the marae, especially in the cities, probably live elsewhere.

Maoritanga	A modern word for Maori culture or the ways and customs of Maori.
Matua	Father.
Moko	The Maori tattoo. In a woman the facial moko is confined to the chin and lips.
Mokopuna	Grandchild.
Ngapuhi	A Maori tribe based in the north of the North Island.
Oneone	Earth, soil.
Pa	Originally a village fortified for defence but now used for any village or settlement.
Pakeha	A New Zealander of European descent.
Piwakawaka	A small and active bird, native to New Zealand, common in the suburban garden. Also known as the fantail.
Pohutukawa	Beautiful coastal tree, (*Metrosideros excelsa*), native to New Zealand, notable for its great spread and its fabulous summer (January-February) display of crimson flowers.
Pouri	Grief, distress, blackness.
Puriri	Hardy tree, (*Vitex lucens*), one of two native New Zealand representatives of the Verbenaceae family, that has a large, spreading canopy. The flowers are produced through most of the year and the red fruit is highly favoured by native birds.
Rata	Tree, (*Metrosideros robusta*), native to New Zealand. Like the pohutukawa, to which it is related, it has profuse crops of brilliant red flowers in the summer, about Christmas time.
Tamaki-makaurau	What the Maori call Auckland and the Auckland region.
Tangi(hanga)	Funeral and wake.

Te Rauparaha	A chief of the a Ngati Toa tribe. A great and famous Maori warrior. (1768–1849)
Tapu	Holy, sacred, sacrosanct, inviolate. In Maori and other Polynesian cultures things or places that are tapu must be left alone.
Tika	Right, apt, appropriate.
Tikanga	The codes, conventions, customs and etiquette of Maori society and culture.
Tui	(*Prosthemadera novaeseelandiae*). A large bird native to the New Zealand bush.
Tupuna	Ancestors.
Wairua	Ghost, spirit.
Weka	A tough, hardy bird, (*Gallirallus australis*), native to New Zealand. Although flightless, it can run very fast. Prefers scrub country at the edge of the forest.
Whanau	Family, extended family.
Whare	A house.
Te whare whakairo	The meeting house of the marae, usually elaborately panelled and carved in the traditional style.
Whenua	Land, ground.

www.ingramcontent.com/pod-product-compliance
Lightning Source LLC
Chambersburg PA
CBHW021922170626
46807CB00007B/2948